THE BELLS
ON FINLAND
STREET

By the same author:

Samantha's Secret Room

THE BELLS
ON FINLAND
STREET

LYN COOK

COVER BY SAM SISCO

Scholastic Canada Ltd.

Scholastic Canada Ltd.
123 Newkirk Road, Richmond Hill, Ontario, Canada
L4C 3G5

Scholastic Inc.
730 Broadway, New York, NY 10003, USA

Ashton Scholastic Limited
Private Bag 1, Penrose, Auckland, New Zealand

Ashton Scholastic Pty Limited
PO Box 579, Gosford, NSW 2250, Australia

Scholastic Publications Ltd.
Holly Walk, Leamington Spa, Warwickshire CV32 4LS, England

Canadian Cataloguing in Publication Data

Cook, Lyn 1918-
    The bells on Finland Street

Rev.ed.
ISBN 0-590-74032-6

I. Title.

PS8505.066B4 1991   jC813'.54   C91-094232-3
PZ7.C66Be 1991

6 5 4 3 2 1   Printed in Canada   1 2 3 4 5/9
Manufactured by Webcom Limited

Preface to the new edition

This story was written many years ago when I was Sudbury's first professional children's librarian. A book begins, another writer has said, by "losing one's heart to something." I lost mine to the city of Sudbury, in its rugged setting, and to its splendid citizens and their children who had come from many corners of the world.

Many changes have taken place in Sudbury, as they have in the rest of the country, since this book was first published more than forty years ago. Environmental concerns have affected that city as they have affected all of us.

But many important things have not changed. There is still an emphasis on people as individuals within a multicultural mosaic, and a sensitivity to the needs of all people to cherish their own and Canada's heritage. Elin Laukka's hopes and dreams remain the same as those of thousands of young Canadians today.

I hope this edition of *The Bells on Finland Street* will make many new friends and find some of the ones it made when I first told Elin's story.

—*Lyn Cook, August 1991*

Preface to the first edition

For reasons of plot and simplification, certain liberties have been taken in this story with the geography of Sudbury and some of its institutions.

All the characters mentioned are purely fictional, but the author hopes the citizens of Sudbury will find in them a tribute to the progressive spirit that has made their city the nickel centre of the world.

Some of the Finnish words and phrases are explained in the telling of Elin's story. Here are the meanings of those that are not explained:

Äiti — Mother

Isä — Father

Suomi — Finland

Laskiainen — Shrove Tuesday, the day before Lent begins

Laskiaispulla — a large, round bun sprinkled with chopped almonds and sugar, eaten on Shrove Tuesday in Finland as we here eat pancakes on that day

Oi Kallis Suomenma — Oh, my precious Finland

"Isä! Isä! Olet onnellisesti perilla!" — "Father! Father! You have arrived safely!"

"Et ole muuttunut, olet sama, Lemmin, kun ennen. Mutta missä on Miina?" — "You haven't changed a bit, Lemmin. But where is Miina?"

"Kotona, Isä, han odattaa kotona" — "At home, Father, she's waiting at home!"

Ilmarinen — a giant blacksmith, the hero of a great Finnish folk story called the Kalevala

limonaatia — a drink made of fresh fruit juices.

—*The Author*

Contents

1. Elin Wants a Friend 1
2. The Skating Fairyland 5
3. Grandfather Won All the Prizes 15
4. Mr. Kurtsheff Says "Yes" 20
5. The Letter 33
6. The Accident 40
7. Äiti Counts Her Money 47
8. Stepan's Concert 54
9. The Music Festival at Last 61
10. Farewell to Skating 74
11. All the Way from Finland 83
12. A Tale of the Trolls 95
13. The Giant Slag's Secret 105
14. Christmas in Finland 113
15. Anna Acts Strangely 120
16. The Wonderful Christmas Gift 129
17. Skating Lessons are Fun 134
18. Why All the Bells Ring 143
19. Carnival Surprises 155
20. Elin Must Be Brave 163
21. The Dress Rehearsal 168
22. "Some Day You Skate for Canada" 173

1

Elin Wants a Friend

"Äiti, if you want somebody for a friend, what do you have to do?" Elin was tracing the picture of a little girl with curly hair on the steamy kitchen window.

"Maybe you do something nice for them. Maybe just smile and they want to be your friend." Äiti had had to think for a while before she answered. While she was thinking she hurried her hot iron over Isä's damp blue work shirt. It made a little sizzling sound that reminded Elin of the little snake she and Stepan had startled among the rocks on the Pinnacle. That was a long time ago! Last summer. And now she was nine, going on ten, a whole year older.

The little blue enamel kettle with the yellow handle whistled on the stove, blew another cloud of steam across the kitchen window and spoiled Elin's picture.

"And who is this now my baby want for friend?" Äiti ironed on sturdily.

"It's Anna. Anna Sadowski," Elin sighed. "Anna's Polish. She sits in front of me at school and she's got the prettiest red hair you ever saw. All curly and short all over her head."

Äiti clucked her tongue gently. "I think my Elin have

lovely hair, too. Such gold hair I do not see on anyone else."

"Who wants yellow hair, anyway?" Elin pulled at one of her pigtails gloomily. "It's just the colour of that old kettle handle. Who wants hair like an old teakettle handle?"

Äiti wet her finger and tested the iron. It hissed greedily, "That kettle cost money, Elin, and we buy for we like the yellow handle. It is pretty. Isä get him in Kresge's."

Elin knew. Everything cost money, and the money always came out of the old glass pickle jar with the green and white label.

"Just the same I wish I had red hair and brown eyes. Then maybe everybody would like me, same as they like Anna." Elin was talking to herself and Äiti scarcely heard, but the teakettle heard and he was so surprised that he blew his lid upside down with a sudden mighty puff of steam. Elin set it right again.

"This Anna, she never say hello to you or any little word?" Äiti folded the shirt and dangled it over the string line stretched from the cupboard to the window.

"Sometimes she smiles at me. But she's got girlfriends of her own, Äiti. There's Yolande Fouillard and Wendy Hill and Elizabeth Graham and Chrissie."

"Well, and what is the matter with little Stepan? He is not good now as friend for you, little one?"

"Oh, Äiti, that's different. I like Stepan a lot and he's fun. I love to go walking with him over the rocks and up to the Pinnacle to sit. But he doesn't like girls much any more." Elin coiled the ends of her fair pigtails around her fingers, to make them curly like Anna's. "I wish Anna would talk to me just once. She must be lots 'n' lots of fun. Everybody plays with Anna at recess. I wish I could."

"And who do you be with in the recess, Elin?"

"Oh, Stepan mostly, but now he plays with the other Ukrainian boys from the Donovan. He says he's getting too old to play with girls. And do you know where Anna lives?" Elin peered through the steam on the window-pane to the spring evening outside, where the rocks of the north country rolled away to the sky, like a great giant sleeping on his side. The giant didn't care where anybody lived. He had the wide blue sky for his roof and thousands of stars to light him to bed.

"Well, where she live?"

"She lives up on the Hill. You know those great big houses?"

Äiti shrugged her shoulders.

"Anna's father's rich, I guess. I heard her telling Chrissie one day that he was foreman out at the mine."

"Same mine where Isä works?" Äiti ironed the wrinkles in her broad forehead with her moist, tired hand.

"Yes, out at Frood." Surely Äiti must see how important Anna was! You couldn't help being important if you lived on the Hill and your father was foreman at the mine. "They must be awful rich. Don't you think so?"

Äiti made the familiar, clucking sound with her tongue and smiled. "It is not all people can be rich, Elin. We do not need the riches. We have Isä and Juhani and our little house on Finland Street. And everybody be in good health. We must give the thanks for that."

In the bedroom off the little kitchen little Juhani whimpered and coughed in his sleep. *It must be awful to be just two years old*, Elin thought, peeking in the bedroom door to see if he were all right. *Nothing to do* but sleep and sleep all the time, and no wonderful people like Anna to dream about.

"Happy! Happy! Happy!" gurgled the little blue enamel teakettle with the yellow handle.

Elin smiled. "I'll do the hankies and the tablecloth, Äiti. They're easy. You sit down and have a rest."

But Äiti had no time to sit down. "I must be getting the food for Isä, when he come home from the mine late." She silenced the singing of the teakettle with cold water from the tap and put on the coffee pot.

It was time for bed as soon as the hankies were done. Elin could hear Äiti's rocking chair creaking a sleepy tune as she snuggled under the covers in her tiny room upstairs.

I'll stay awake until Isä comes home, she thought. *I'll make believe Anna is my friend. Anna will be laughing out in the schoolyard, and I'll smile, and then . . .*

Elin was asleep.

2

The Skating Fairyland

"Maybe you do something nice for them. Maybe just smile and they want to be your friend." That's what Äiti had said last night. *"Maybe you do something nice for them."* But what could Elin Laukka, who lived on Finland Street, do for Anna Sadowski who lived on the Hill? Anna always did everything for herself.

Elin practised smiling in arithmetic class and the teacher saw her and smiled back. She smiled in geography class, while she was drawing a map of Northern Ontario. It was when she was printing Sudbury on her map in big round letters that it happened.

She heard a soft little plunk and looked on the floor. There was an eraser, scurrying down the aisle like a little red goblin! She stuck out her foot and stopped it. And there was *Anna* stretching out her hand for it. It was Anna's eraser! She had rescued *Anna's* eraser! Maybe now Anna would speak to her. But no . . . Anna smiled a thank you and tossed her red curls over her notebook. Elin began to work on her map of Northern Ontario again. Under Sudbury she printed Nickel with her red crayon. But she didn't smile when she printed it. She felt rather sad.

But after four she forgot to feel sad. It was spring. The earth smelled like things growing. Elin sniffed the spring air and poked along on her way home from school. There were the rock hills all dressed up in a misty green gown! *That's the silver birches in bud,* she thought. *Spring's here. If I listen I may hear a robin.* And there — what was that little, shiny, red thing, almost buried in the earth at the edge of the sidewalk like a great glistening seed? An alley! One of the boys had lost an alley in the mud.

"Elin! Elin! Wait for me! I'm coming!"

Elin turned, startled. It was Anna! She was racing along, sweater coat unbuttoned and creeping down from her sturdy shoulders, schoolbag plump-plumping against her bare legs.

Plump! Plump! That was what Elin's heart sounded like inside her. Her face felt all hot. *This is how I wanted it to happen,* she thought. And now what did she want to do? She wanted to run away! To change herself into the little red alley and bury herself in the mud!

She drew a deep breath and smiled. "Hello, Anna. I didn't know you came my way home. Don't you live up on the Hill?"

"Sure I do." Anna puffed and jerked her sweater coat up over her shoulders. "But Tuesday's the day I take my skating lesson at the arena. Do you skate, Elin?"

"Oh, yes, in the winter I do. I go skating on the lake when the ice gets thick enough. Sometimes it's too cold, though."

"Oh, no! That's not the kind of skating I mean." Anna heaved at her schoolbag a little importantly. "I mean figure skating. Didn't you go to the Carnival last year?"

The Carnival at the Skating Club Arena! Now Elin

knew. She shook her head, shyly. "We were going to go, Isä and Äiti and me." She hesitated. "Well, then we just didn't," she ended lamely.

Please, please don't let Anna ask why. Elin remembered so well. Isä had come home from the mine one night, very excited. "There is big talk of Carnival in town. First Carnival Sudbury have!"

"Carnival!" Äiti had flung herself upon him with a shout of joy. "Oh, Lemmin! I have not see the Carnival since I leave the good Finland. We must go, Lemmin. We all go!" Äiti rushed to the little glass pickle jar and counted out the money. There was enough for all three of them. Juhani could stay with Mrs. Venna.

But Mr. Kurtsheff's grocery bill had come in the mail the next day. Äiti couldn't believe they had eaten so much! She counted out the money that was left and shrugged her shoulders. Maybe some other time . . .

"What street do you live on, Elin?" Anna didn't like silence. What was the use of walking along saying nothing when there was so much to say?

"Finland Street. At the end by the rocks."

"Oh, that's the funny little street where all the houses are the same, isn't it?"

Little fires flared up in Elin's cheeks. She felt hot all over. Why did she have to live on a street where all the houses were the same? Where every tiny clapboard dwelling had the same little verandah and the same little back porch? Anna lived in a brick house. Mrs. Venna went to clean up there on the Hill sometimes. "Two bathrooms I scrub!" she complained to Äiti over the back fence. "And the silver I clean . . . " Äiti had made her little clucking sound.

"Gee, you've got pretty hair," Anna was saying.

Maybe that would make Elin feel better. Elin's face was so red, but Anna didn't really know why. People were funny sometimes. "Your hair's just like sunshine," Anna marvelled again. There now. That's what Yolande Fouillard would say. Yolande was just about the most polite person Anna knew. It must be tiresome to think up nice things to say to people all the time! But Elin was smiling again.

"I like yours a lot better." Elin gazed enviously at the short red curls. "I think you've got the prettiest hair I ever saw."

"Oh, I don't know." Nobody had ever said that to Anna before. All the boys called her "Carrots," and even Pop called her "Rusty." But Elin had said she had the prettiest hair she ever saw! "Say, Elin." Anna sidled closer and linked her arm with Elin's. "Why don't you come over to the Arena and watch us take our lesson from Mr. Crane? That'd be fun if you've never seen anyone figure skate. It doesn't last long. Will you come?"

Would she come? Elin forgot about Äiti waiting for her to look after Juhani while she got the supper! She forgot about Isä trudging in from the long day at the mine, tired, and hungry for his cabbage roll and ham. "Oh, Anna, I'd just love to!" she gasped.

"Well, don't you think you'd better run home and tell your Mom where you're going first?"

Elin nodded. Anna was wonderful. She thought of everything! They skipped down the street, arm in arm — two friends. There was Mr. Kurtsheff, leaning against the door of his grocery store in the late afternoon sun. His big, fat cigar nearly leaped out of his mouth in surprise as they flew past him down Finland Street.

Wait till I tell him about Anna, Elin thought importantly.

"I'll wait on the front steps," Anna suggested, when they reached the little house at the end of the street near the rocks.

"I won't be a minute, Anna." Elin dashed out again in less time than that! "I can go, Anna. Äiti says I can go!"

"What's Äiti?"

"That's Finnish for mother. Äiti says I'm to be back in an hour."

"C'mon then. Let's hurry." Anna grabbed her hand and they sped up Finland Street. Mr. Kurtsheff saw them when they passed the corner again. He pushed his big white cap back on his head and scratched his shiny bald spot thoughtfully. Elin could almost hear him say, "Mine goodness! Vat's goink on here mit mine friend Elin?"

It was just like the story of Ali Baba and the Forty Thieves when they reached the big brass gates of the arena. Elin whispered, "Open Sesame," and Anna heard her.

"What did you say?" she asked Elin as an attendant in a blue uniform opened the gates and let them into the cool darkness.

Elin blushed. "It's just from a fairy-tale all about a magic cave that opens when somebody says, 'Open Sesame.' "

"And what's inside?" Anna guided Elin along the corridors in the darkness.

"Secret treasure."

"Secret treasure, huh? I never read any books much. Only school books. I don't have time. There's too many other things to do." Anna started to run. "Hi, kids!"

"Hi, Anna!" Three girls called loudly from the bench at the far end under the spotlight. "Where've you been? We've been waiting . . . " They stopped short when they saw Elin.

"I brought Elin to see us take our lesson today. I have to go and change. You wait here, Elin, and the kids will tell you about figure skating." Anna whirled away, a flurry of curls, sweater coat and schoolbag.

"What did she mean, tell you about figure skating?" Wendy Hill peered sharply at Elin over the heavy, black-rimmed spectacles that straddled her freckled nose in a surprised sort of way. "Can't you skate?"

"I can't do the kind of skating you do. I only skate with my father on the lake sometimes."

"Well, you should be able to figure skate. Everybody should be able to figure skate." That was like Wendy. She was always telling people what they should do. Not that anybody paid any attention. Even if she was ten years old. But people paid attention when Wendy's father spoke. He was very clever and knew all about money and adding up huge sums in the bank. "Well, anyway," Wendy would say when she made a mistake in arithmetic at school, "my Dad's the best adder in Sudbury, and he's boss of the bank!"

"Of course everybody can't figure skate, Wendy." Yolande arranged her black hair neatly over her shoulders and gave Wendy a warning poke. "Come and sit down here with us on the bench, Elin," she smiled.

Then it was true what Anna had told her about Yolande on the way over to the arena. "She's just about the politest person I've ever seen," Anna had said. "Sometimes she acts as if she's years 'n years old, like your mother or your auntie." But that wasn't really surprising, Elin thought, as she moved over to the bench and sat down. Yolande had lots of brothers and sisters and had to be a mother to them most of the time. Just the same as Elin was mother to Juhani when Äiti was busy.

What short skirts Wendy and Yvonne wore! And the skates! The beautiful white figure-skating shoes! She had never seen anything so graceful. They weren't a bit like the ones Isä had brought home from Rickman's Second-Hand Store for her.

She and Stepan had been playing jacks on the kitchen floor the night he brought the skates in. "Look! Look what Isä have for his baby!" he had shouted gaily. "Gosh, they're boy's skates," Stepan had laughed, but Äiti had shushed him with a quick slap on the seat of his pants. "Skates is skates the same," she declared proudly. Isä hovered over Elin while she tried one on. "Does it fit?" he wanted to know, anxiously. Elin was glad when Juhani had tried to put the other skate on his head because everybody laughed and didn't notice that she winced a little because it pinched her toes. "Ho, ho!" Isä had shouted. "That is good place to have the skate, Juhani, on the head! That is most like the place where Isä skate if he ever put the skate on and try! On his head! Ho, ho!"

"Have a piece of candy, Elin?" Elizabeth Graham helped herself first to a big, round candy from a large bag. Elizabeth was always eating. She even took candy to school and nibbled on it when the teacher wasn't looking. One day she had left her desk to write memory-work on the blackboard, and there, sticking to the pleats of her black skirt, was a large yellow gumdrop! Nothing would ever stop Elizabeth from eating candy. Nothing would make her good in arithmetic, either, and she was eleven and her father was Mr. Graham, the mining engineer.

"Aren't you ready yet?" Here was Anna back from the dressing-room. How slow the other girls were! Anna was all ready and they were still dawdling about, lacing their boots. Anna didn't like to wait. There was so much to do and she might miss something.

Elin couldn't take her eyes from Anna's short, scarlet skirt. And the way it shimmered in the shining steel of her skates, and reflected in the ice around her in a scarlet pool.

"Now then, young ladies. Out on the ice at once, please!" Mr. Crane's jolly face was almost as red as Anna's skirt as he skimmed up the ice, clapping his hands, briskly. The blades made a little singing sound as the girls tumbled on to the ice. Elin was left alone, Elizabeth's bag of candy beside her on the bench.

But then she forgot the rows of empty benches rising silently in the darkness above her. She forgot the tiny house on the street where all the tiny houses were the same. She forgot that Äiti had asked her to come home in an hour . . .

At a sign from the round-faced Mr. Crane, the girls sped down the ice like four swallows, weaving beautiful arcs in the dim light.

"It's perfect," breathed Elin. "It's like the gulls flying off the shore of Lake Ramsay."

One! Two! Three!

That was the town clock calling out the hours down by the post office. Elin counted five. Five o'clock! *Time to go home!* Whatever would Äiti be thinking? Juhani would be crying, or pulling out all the pots and pans from the lower cupboard, while Äiti was trying to get supper. And Isä would soon be home, very soon, hungry and tired!

She slipped along the edge of the ice in the half-darkness and groped for the door. She turned to take one last look. The girls were gliding towards her, hand in hand, their skirts, scarlet, white and blue, swirling about them like one great splendid flag.

Anna's the best! she thought gleefully. *And Anna's going to be my friend!*

She hurried through the brass gates and out on the street. Everything looked so drab after the skating fairyland she had left. But if she squinted her eyes just a little against the evening sun, a wonderful thing happened. A carpet of gold spread over all the world around her. Even the old freight car, down on the siding at the railway station, was a golden coach, and she was Cinderella, running to leap into it.

She flew, as quickly as her thin legs would carry her, down past the market square, over the slope beside the Church of Christ the King, down across the road past the sprawling hospital, and up the hill toward Finland Street. Fat old Mr. Kurtsheff was humped up in front of his store like a big penguin bird, with a cigar for a beak and a rumpled white apron-breast. He waved and croaked genially, "In big hurry, Elin girl?"

Elin waved happily. *Poor Mr. Kurtsheff*, she thought. *He's never seen figure skating. He doesn't even know I'm going to be the most wonderful figure skater in the whole, wide world! Poor Mr. Kurtsheff!*

That was it! *She* would learn to figure skate and *she* would win all the prizes. How proud of her Anna would be then! And Äiti and Isä, and even Juhani when he got bigger! A great figure skater! As she raced along, she felt herself skimming across the ice in the bird-like motion she had just seen. She gave three quick skips of pure joy.

Then she was on Finland Street and all the little white houses danced past her as she hastened home; the little white houses with their tiny front verandahs and their tiny back porches all the same. There was Mrs. Salo's and there was Mrs. Haaki's. There was Mrs. Ronskainen's and there was Mrs. Venna's. And suddenly there was home. She bounded up the steps and into the house.

3

Grandfather Won
All the Prizes

"What a happy face my Elin have!" Äiti was stirring the soup in the red pot with a long-handled spoon. Round and round.

"It's a late face," Elin panted, her cheeks puffed out like the sides of the little red pot. "Äiti, I'm sorry. I forgot the time. I was with Anna and . . . "

"It do not matter, little one." Elin was glad to see Äiti was smiling. "But table is to be setted and Juhani's hands and face need bad the wash." Äiti clucked her tongue softly at Juhani's grubby, tear-stained little face. "Where is all your smiles go, baby?"

"I'll make you a new face, Juhani." Elin ran to get the washcloth. Juhani wailed. He didn't like soap and water! Elin felt as grown up as Yvonne as she blotted up his tears with the frayed yellow washcloth.

"This is my own little skating rink," she played, as she slithered the blue cotton cloth on the kitchen table. "And here we go, Anna and I, swishing down the ice!" She skated the red and white salt and pepper shakers across the blue cloth, and then opened the drawer of the cupboard by the window where the knives and forks lived. There they were, twinkling like silver skates. Elin looked out of the window to see what was happening on Finland Street.

"Oh, Äiti, here comes Isä already!"

Under the dim arcs of the street lamps, in little groups of twos and threes, the miners were coming home from the shift, each carrying his black lunch pail. Heads bent together in talk, caps pushed back. Not much like skating. Isä's step sounded heavily on the verandah. "And how is my Elin tonight?" He set the black lunch pail on the kitchen cupboard, ready for Äiti to fill for morning. Elin scarcely heard him. She was busy being a great figure skater.

"Elin no eating her soup? Is very good soup, too. My little girl playing too hard, eh? Too tired to eat now?" Isä shook his finger at Elin as she picked at the spiced cabbage roll on her plate.

"She is play with Anna Sadowski. Now she is happy I guess. Anna! Anna! Anna! That is all the word I hear. Always Anna!" But Äiti looked pleased.

Playing! How could Äiti call the wonderful figure skating playing? But that's right. Äiti was like Mr. Kurtsheff. Äiti hadn't seen the figure skating. And had Elin ever said she'd be happy if she had Anna for a friend? So she had! But how could she ever be really happy again unless she learned to figure skate?

Äiti clucked her tongue. She was taking Elin's plate from the table. "Is not good for you, Elin. You must eat to be big, strong girl like your Isä."

Isä laughed and reached for another piece of bread. "You're hearing that, Elin? One day you be big, strong girl like me, will you?" Isä laughed again.

What's the use of that? I don't want to be a miner like

Isä, Elin thought. *I want to be a great figure skater.* She drew a little skate on the tablecloth with her pudding spoon. "Isä, would it cost a lot of money to take skating lessons, please?"

Isä laid down his knife and fork. "Lessons, Elin? Why take the lessons? How often do we go skating on the lake together, eh? When the ice is thick?" He threw back his head and chuckled. "Why, it is summer and my baby talk of skating!"

Elin was impatient. "No, Isä, that's not the kind of skating I mean. To learn to figure skate. That wouldn't cost a lot of money, would it?"

Äiti sailed in on a gay bubble of laughter with the puddings. "She asks to figure skate, Lemmin!" Elin listened a little harder, for Äiti was speaking in Finnish. "It's what our wonderful Isä used to do!"

"You mean Grandfather, Äiti? Did Grandfather do it?"

"Yes, yes, little one! He's in big fair like we have in Suomi in wintertime. He win big prize for the skating!"

"Äiti! You never told me!" Think of it. Grandfather a figure skater and Äiti hadn't said a word!

"Whoosh he go! Like big bird across the ice and everybody clap and shout loud." Äiti's pudding was forgotten. Her eyes sparkled with joy.

She's got a new face, Elin marvelled secretly. *Just like the new shining face I gave Juhani with the washcloth!*

Äiti was still remembering. "Then when he win the big prize he go to great city Helsinki to skate with more man and lady and he is the champion there, too!"

"What's champion mean, Isä?" Elin leaned eagerly across the table.

"Champion is the best one of all, Elin. He get the prize."

"Oh, he was good, Isä! And so clever!" Äiti leaned her elbows on the table and cradled her head in her rough, red hands.

Äiti's just like me, Elin thought. *When I was eating my cabbage roll I wasn't really here. I was being a figure skater. Äiti isn't really here now. She's in Finland.*

Elin's heart was doing a hop-skip-jump. It was almost too much. Her very own grandfather! And he had won prizes because he was so good. *Prizes!* Just wait till she told that to Anna and Elizabeth and Wendy. Her own grandfather was a champion!

"Those were good days, Lemmin." Tears glistened in Äiti's eyes.

"Did you ever go to the carnivals, Äiti?" Elin asked eagerly.

"Till I come here I never miss one in our village, Elin." The words tumbled from Äiti's lips as if she were saying memory-work. "Many month before, we make the plan for the good time we have. That is on the day of Laskiainen. The Shrove Tuesday, they say here. We all go down to lake and watch finest men in village do the skate and the ski, and we give big clap to the best man. And our Isä was always best man. Always. Then we go home and eat special meal of all things bake just for that day. And very special is the Laskiaispulla."

"I know, that's pancakes." Elin teetered on the edge of her chair with excitement. "Did you ever figure skate, Äiti?"

"No, little one. My Äiti, she think it is better for the little girls to learn how to be good wife and mother. We skate on the pond after school is over, and go ride on the pulkka across the fields in snow. But no fancy skate for your Äiti."

"And didn't any girls figure skate in Finland, Äiti? Any at all?"

"Oh, yes, some girls do. I have cousin who skate almost as good as Isä. But she do not win the prize." The corners of Äiti's mouth were trembling. She pulled her faded red apron up to her eyes. Elin could feel her own lips pucker. A funny lump was growing in her throat.

Isä leaned across the table and laid his big hand gently over Äiti's. "It is not good for the child, Miina, these tears. It is good to have the glad memories, wife."

"Down! Down!" Juhani was shouting orders in a captain's voice, from his high chair.

Elin looked at Isä and Äiti. They hadn't even heard Juhani. They were just sitting there, silent. Juhani jumped into her arms with a gurgle and she carried him into the bedroom.

When she crept back into the kitchen they were standing quietly at the kitchen window, Isä's arm close around Äiti's shoulders. They couldn't be looking at the sleeping giant, because only Elin knew about him lying out there under the stars. No . . . Elin knew. They were looking far over the sea to Finland.

Elin sighed. She stole back to the bedroom on tiptoe. *Just the same,* she thought, *Isä didn't say a word about the skating lessons.*

4

Mr. Kurtsheff says "Yes"

"Why don't you take the lessons from Mr. Crane, too, if you like figure skating so much, Elin?" Anna was walking home from school, her arm flung about Elin's shoulders. "I bet Mr. Crane would let you in, even if it is late."

Elin thought of Äiti, painfully counting out the pennies from the little pickle jar for a pound of sausage. She shook her head. "Isä says it costs a lot of money to take lessons, Anna. We haven't got a lot of money. Isä says we must be happy that we're all well and that we have a home and things to eat. Some people don't."

"You mean some people haven't got enough to eat?" Anna slowed down her steps, her eyes two startled question marks in her round face. "I don't believe it."

"It must be true 'cause that's what Isä says," Elin maintained stoutly. "Isä never says anything that isn't true. Anyway, I can't take lessons. It's too much money."

"Who's taking lessons?" They both whirled round. There were Wendy Hill and Yolande Fouillard, running along swinging their coats over their arms in the heat of the afternoon. "Did I hear somebody talking about lessons? Who's going to take lessons?" Wendy shoved her wiry little body between Anna and Elin.

"It's Elin. She can't take skating lessons because she hasn't got any money," Anna sighed. "I wish I had lots of money. I'd give her some."

Wendy pushed her spectacles straight with the tip of a grimy finger. She peered knowingly over them at Elin. "Maybe Mr. Crane wouldn't let you take lessons, anyway, even if you had the money. Nobody from Finland Street takes lessons."

"Don't you think he would, even if I had the money?" Elin was startled with this new idea. "Doesn't Mr. Crane like Finnish people or something?"

"I never said that," Wendy sniffed. "But you live on Finland Street. Your Mum and Dad came from Finland."

"Well, what's wrong with that, anyway?" Yolande politely elbowed her way to Elin's side and slipped her arm through Elin's. "After all, once upon a time, 'way back, my people came from France. And do you know what?"

"No, what?"

"My father says a long time ago we used to be dukes and duchesses. In France I mean."

"Humph, that's nothing." Wendy's eyes widened a little behind the spectacles. "My Dad says we're descended from the Kings of Ireland!"

"The Kings of Ireland!" Anna stood with her hands on her hips and feet sturdily apart. "Well. All I know is . . . my Pop's a Pole!"

Kings and dukes and . . . just a Pole! Wendy looked at Yolande and began to giggle. Yolande giggled, too. Suddenly there they were, all shaking with laughter, especially Wendy, who shook so hard that her spectacles flew off and bounced on the ground. Yolande, Elin and

Anna bounded to pick them up. Their heads bumped together and that only made them laugh harder than ever.

Wendy wiped the tears from her eyes before she pushed the spectacles back over her nose. "Say," she turned eagerly to Elin, "you know what you ought to do? You ought to get a job and earn the money to take the lessons."

"Get a job? I can't do anything, though. Where would I get one?"

"You could be a baby-sitter. My big sister's a baby-sitter lots of times. And that's not hard."

"I'm not old enough to be a baby-sitter. You have to be in high school for that."

"What do you mean, not old enough?" Anna smiled. "You're always telling me you have to look after Juhani. That's baby-sitting, isn't it?"

"That's different," Elin insisted. "He's my own brother and I don't get paid for that." She stopped at the corner of the street. "Well, I have to go into Mr. Kurtsheff's store for Äiti. Goodbye, Anna! Goodbye, Yolande!" Then she called over her shoulder. "Goodbye, Wendy!"

"Goodbye, Finland!" Wendy grinned and waved in a very friendly fashion. "Goodbye, Finland!"

Elin whipped up the steps and into Mr. Kurtsheff's store. To think that a little while ago she hadn't liked Wendy at all. Now Wendy was her friend, too. She was really lots of fun!

The captivating smell, a rare mixture of spiced meat, licorice candy and Mr. Kurtsheff, greeted her like an old friend. Mrs. Venna was leaning over the counter chatting with the fat storekeeper.

"Oh, I know it must be keeping you busy, Mr.

Kurtsheff. All this work and nobody to help. If I was more young I would be here myself to earn money."

Mr. Kurtsheff sighed deeply and planted his fat elbows on the counter. A smile sparkled on Elin's face. Mr. Kurtsheff's elbows always made her smile, because, if she screwed up her eyes tightly, she could see two funny faces on them where the plumpness fell in lines and dimples, almost like the chubby faces of two little ladies.

"I got to get somebody, Mrs. Venna, that I'm knowing," Mr. Kurtsheff complained. "It's that I'm getting old and this is big store. Then the kids is out from the school on summer holiday and whish! Every five minute they is in here, for the ice cream cone, the candy bar." He raised his hand where the plump skin crinkled like the soft folds of a tiny silk gown, and wiped his shining forehead. "Oh vell, mebbe somebody come along who wants the job." He looked around and noticed Elin. "Vell, it's mine Elin from Finland Street. Vat is you wanting today, Elin?"

"Äiti wants a pound of sausage, please, Mr. Kurtsheff, the long kind." She stood quietly while Mr. Kurtsheff took down a long roll of thick sausage from the rack behind him and began to wrap it. How firm and heavy that big lump of meat must feel in his stubby fingers. It would be fun to help in a store, almost like playing shop with Stepan, only there would be real meat and pickles to sell, instead of pebbles and empty honey pails. But Mr. Kurtsheff had just said he wanted help in the store! And Wendy had told her she should get a job to earn money. Maybe . . . *I wonder if I'm too little,* she thought. *I guess nobody would want me. But maybe they would. I could ask Mr. Kurtsheff, anyway.* Why didn't Mrs. Venna pick up her parcels and go, so that she could talk to Mr. Kurtsheff alone? But Mrs. Venna was still there, leaning over the counter, looking over the rows of tinned goods on the shelves to complete her order.

"Thank you, Mr. Kurtsheff." Elin took the parcel of sausage in her hand and started for the door. Then she turned quickly. "Mr. Kurtsheff, you'll be open tonight, won't you?"

"Always open till nine, Elin. Always here."

"Thanks, Mr. Kurtsheff." She bounded away down the street towards home, her mind a merry-go-round of exciting thoughts. *Tonight I'll go back and ask him,* she thought. *Maybe there's just a little hope he might want me. Maybe.*

"Äiti, may I please go down to the store for a few minutes?" Elin hung the dish towel across the rack and piled Juhani's toys up neatly in the corner of the kitchen.

"There is nothing we need. For what are you go to store, please?"

Elin traced the pattern of a slender skate on the window. "Well, I just thought I'd like to go to see Mr. Kurtsheff. He always likes to talk to me, Äiti."

"Why, it is only this afternoon you see him, when you get sausage for supper." Äiti clucked her tongue. "I think you just want to have walk, maybe. Run now and home again before the dark come."

Elin did not wait for a second invitation. She whisked out of the door, down the steps and in no time at all found Mr. Kurtsheff sitting on the front stoop of his store, as usual. His wooden chair was tilted back against the store front and a big cigar hung from his mouth. He must have been dreaming for a long time. Perhaps he was even asleep, for all the ashes from the cigar had dribbled down on the bib of his apron, and lay there like a landslide of tiny rocks on a monstrous white mountain. Elin stole up softly beside him. "Hello, Mr. Kurtsheff. How are you tonight?"

Mr. Kurtsheff jumped and blinked his eyes owlishly. He coughed at the sudden puff of smoke he breathed in and almost lost his balance on the chair. "Hello, hello. Vat's this we're having now? Oh, it's you, Elin girl. Your Mama wanting something, mebbe, eh?"

"Nope, not tonight, Mr. Kurtsheff. I just came down to say hello, that's all."

"Vell, vell. That is very nice, I'm sure. Hello. It's been hot day and I'm tired all out. Your Papa and Mama okay, Elin?"

"Fine, thank you, Mr. Kurtsheff." Elin sat down on the step and folded her hands primly in her lap. She looked around Mr. Kurtsheff like a little mouse peeking out of his hole in the wall. Elin cleared her throat. "Mr. Kurtsheff," she began stiffly, "I was in the store this afternoon."

Mr. Kurtsheff digested this information carefully and chewed on the end of his cigar. "Vell, that I'm knowing, Elin. So you was in the store this afternoon. So what is so strange about that now?"

"I was here when Mrs. Venna was here."

"Yes, that is right. Then vat is strange about Mrs. Venna and Elin girl being in the store both together at same time? That means more business for Kurtsheff. That is good." Mr. Kurtsheff's apron heaved in a deep sigh of satisfaction.

Elin pulled at her pigtails and took a long, slow breath. "You must work awful hard, Mr. Kurtsheff, having nobody to help you in the store and everything. You must get awful tired all by yourself."

"Work is vat I am used to, Elin girl. Anyway there is plenty of me to do it, not so?" Mr. Kurtsheff's big body rumbled with laughter like a sleeping volcano.

"But you said, well, maybe somebody would come along who wanted the job!"

Now she had said it and not the way she had meant to at all! She folded her hands again and tried to remember how Äiti sat when Mrs. Venna came to call on Wednesday afternoons. "It wouldn't be a very hard job." Elin gazed hard at the scuffed toes of her shoes.

Mr. Kurtsheff winked slyly. He pursed up his lips and frowned. "Vell now, I am seeing vat you mean. Yes, Elin. I was thinking mebbe of having in help for little while in afternoons. Mebbe nice young boy like Stepan is wanting to work after school, not so? You thinking Stepan would like to work, eh? Or mebbe some other boy?"

"But boys like to have fun after school, Mr. Kurtsheff. They play ball and swim, and Stepan even goes to learn Ukrainian dances at the hall. I don't think Stepan would ever want to work after school." Elin pulled so hard at her pigtails that the blue ribbons fell off and she struggled to tie them on again.

"Vell, mebbe you is knowing another little boy who is wanting work? Is that not so, Elin? Mebbe you tell me his name, not so?"

"Well, not exactly, Mr. Kurtsheff." Elin finished tying the second blue ribbon.

"Mebbe little boy by name of Elin Laukka, not so?" Mr. Kurtsheff exploded in a cascade of chuckles over his own joke.

Mr. Kurtsheff knew all the time why she had come!

"Oh, Mr. Kurtsheff! If you'd let me work for you I'd be so glad! And I'd work terribly hard, honest I would!"

Elin tugged anxiously at his trouser leg.

"And don't your Mama need you at home, Elin, after school?"

"She wouldn't need me if I had other work to do and was earning some money. You see, Mr. Kurtsheff, it's terribly important. It's for lessons."

"Oh, so, for lessons!" Mr. Kurtsheff brought his chair down to the floor with an abrupt thump. "And vat is these lessons? You're getting the lessons at school, not so?"

"Oh, it's not school lessons, Mr. Kurtsheff. It's fig-ure-skating lessons. Anna takes and Elizabeth Graham takes and Wendy and Yolande and all the rest. And Mr. Kurtsheff, do you know what?"

"No, vat?"

"Some day I'm going to be a really great skater, like the people you read about in the papers. Oh, Mr. Kurtsheff! I want the lessons so much. I want to be able to fly just like a bird, too! It must be just wonderful! And Mr. Kurtsheff, I'd work awfully hard."

"Vell, mebbe it's good idea." Mr. Kurtsheff smiled down into her blue eyes and nodded his head slowly, considering. "Vell, mebbe would be okay. Ven you start back to school, Elin girl?"

"We get out at the end of June and we don't go back till September." Elin's heart was leaping like a jack-rab-bit. "I could come after school till we stop, Mr. Kurtsheff."

Mr. Kurtsheff teetered back and forth on his wooden chair. "Okay if you start tomorrow then, after school? You're looking after the candy and ice cream counter. Okay?"

"Oh, Mr. Kurtsheff!" Elin leaned over to hug him, nearly toppled both him and the chair over, and then hurried off down Finland Street, calling behind her, "I'll be back tomorrow afternoon after school!"

Isä was sitting on the front steps reading the *Sudbury Star* when Elin sped up the pathway. "Well, and what is all this smile for, baby? Why is there so much happiness?"

"Oh, Isä, the most wonderful thing has happened!" Elin flung herself down on the step beside him. "Maybe I'll be able to take lessons after all! And all by myself, too!"

"Lessons? And what do you learn, Elin girl?" Isä folded up his newspaper.

Elin gasped. Isä could not have forgotten so soon! "You . . . you remember, Isä. Figure skating! I told you about it the other day, when I'd been to see Anna skate at the arena. Oh, Isä, wouldn't it be wonderful if I could skate, too?"

"And how is my girl learn to skate? I think we say there is no money for the lesson, Elin. That cost much money." Isä shook his head and patted her hand as if to comfort her.

Elin shook her hand free. "No, no, Isä! I got a job! I'm going to earn the money all by myself!"

"My Elin got a job? Now where?"

"Mr. Kurtsheff's hired me and I'm going to work there after four till school stops, and then every afternoon. Oh, Isä, maybe I can take lessons, can't I?"

"So, my girl is work for the lessons. That is good. That is very good." Isä smiled proudly up at the rock hills where the long summer evening was fading to twilight.

"I'll save all of it, Isä, and then maybe it won't take long till I have enough."

"And where will you keep it, this money from store?

All in one good, safe place?"

Elin nodded. "I got an old shoebox upstairs. I'll keep it in that and put it under the bed. Every time Mr. Kurtsheff pays me, I'll put the money in."

"Now, Elin," Isä began, "I do not like this idea of shoebox. There is far better thing. If you work you must go to bank and put money there. In that place it will be safe."

"Go to that big building near Rath's Drug Store and leave my money there? Maybe they'd lose it, Isä. I couldn't do that."

"These banks," Isä laughed, "they never lose the money, Elin. It is very safe there. When the first pay come, you and me, we go down to the bank and put in the money. That is wise thing to do."

"But Äiti keeps her money in the little glass pickle jar, Isä."

"Yes, Elin, that is different thing. Äiti spends all the time the money. One day there is money in pickle jar. The next day come a bill, and there is no money in pickle jar."

"Well," Elin nodded doubtfully, "I guess if you think it's all right, Isä, I'll do it."

The first afternoon at Mr. Kurtsheff's store was exciting. She had scarcely taken her place behind the counter when Mr. Kurtsheff called to her from the meat table. "Here is the first customer, Elin. Wait on him, please."

Elin looked fearfully toward the door and then she laughed. "Why, it's only Stepan. Do you want something, Stepan?"

"What are you doing here, Elin, behind the counter?"

Stepan swept his black hair out of his eyes with a grubby hand.

"I'm working for Mr. Kurtsheff now, Stepan."

"Working? What for?" Stepan smudged the glass counter with his dusty elbows.

"Ha! Ha! That is big secret!" Mr. Kurtsheff winked from the table where he was slicing sausage meat, and Elin giggled. "It is secret we not tell, eh, Elin? A secret of *Elin & Kurtsheff!*"

"Can I guess what it is? What letter does it begin with?"

"We're not telling," Elin laughed. *I'll tell him tomorrow, though,* she thought. *Stepan's my friend and I want him to know about me going to be a famous skater.*

"Gee!" Stepan gazed at Elin with new respect. "Well, I want an ice cream cone, please. You can put in as much ice cream as you want, too," he added hopefully.

"One scoop to the customer, please, Elin," Mr. Kurtsheff warned her. "Of course, to the friends, mebbe a little bigger scoop, eh?"

Elin nodded and took the scoop firmly in her hand and dipped it into the freezer. She balanced the white ice cream carefully on the cone, where it was poised like the tremendous white wig on the French lady in the story book.

"I only got a quarter," Stepan announced, licking the cone with gusto. "I have to go into the drug store for Mom with the rest."

Elin gazed down at the money in the cupped palm of her hand. She had seen people making change lots of times and it always looked so easy. But there were all those funny keys on the money machine. She moved slowly to the cash register. Mr. Kurtsheff waddled his fat body, turtle-fashion, over beside her. "Now comes the time ven we learn new things, Elin. Here is how we get the money." He showed her how to open the register and press the right keys. "Now vat is change for Stepan? He is buying ice cream and he is giving a quarter. So?"

Elin screwed up her face in an agony of mental arithmetic. "It's twenty!" she announced triumphantly. "We have to give him twenty cents!"

"That's good girl, Elin," Mr. Kurtsheff smiled. "It don't take long before you got it all in one flash."

"Huh, that was easy, anyway." Stepan held out his grimy palm for the money. "I could have told you that right off. Know what I'm going to do to earn money this summer?"

"What, Stepan?"

"I'm going to catch minnows and sell them to the American tourists who come here to fish. I'll bet I make a lot of money, too, more than you do here." Stepan's tongue curled around the ice cream cone.

"Do they always come in with a lot of money?" Elin turned a troubled face to Mr. Kurtsheff when Stepan had gone.

"Mine goodness, no. Most often it is the nickel for the ice cream cone and that's all. Now if you vas in mine Vienna . . . "

"Did you really live in Vienna once, Mr. Kurtsheff, away across the ocean?" Elin climbed up on the high stool to hear about Vienna. Mr. Kurtsheff leaned his dimpling elbows comfortably on the counter.

"Ah, mine Vienna! That is the city. And mine father. The best butcher in all Vienna. Ah, that was the time." He sighed and pushed his white cap back on his head. "Mine father was fine man, Elin. I'm wishing he is here

5

The Letter

"Today is the payday," Mr. Kurtsheff announced briskly on Friday night, sealing a brown envelope with a lick of his vast tongue. "Is all yours, Elin girl." He laid the envelope on the counter beside her. "Is all yours for one week's pay in Kurtsheff's store."

"Oh, thank you, Mr. Kurtsheff!" Elin finished washing the ice cream scoop and then tore the envelope open. Inside the quarters and dimes jingled like bells.

"Now what you do mit all that money, Elin girl? You rich, eh?"

"It's all going in the bank, Mr. Kurtsheff, every bit of it." The money rattled on the counter as Elin tipped the envelope.

"Vat you saying? And you not spending one cent in Kurtsheff's store?" Mr. Kurtsheff flung up his arms in dismay. "Kurtsheff is soon closing the shop mit no business!" Elin could see the twinkle in his round eyes. She laughed.

Mr. Kurtsheff reached his fat red hand over and picked up some pieces of silver. He laid them on the counter. "There is one hour's work of mine Elin," he smiled, pointing to the money. Then he singled out some more. "And that is another hour's work of mine Elin."

"You mean that's what I get every hour I work here?" Elin pointed to one of the piles of money lined up before her. "You mean I get paid for every hour, just like Isä and all the men who work in the mine?" Just wait till Isä heard this news! All the splendid hours she had spent with Mr. Kurtsheff in the store were lying before her here on the counter.

"Every pile means one hour's work," Elin explained later to Isä at home, arranging the money just as Mr. Kurtsheff had done, in little silver mounds across the kitchen table.

"That is much money for little girl." Isä's eyes smiled. "Now tomorrow Isä is on night shift. We go down to bank when I get home and put money in."

"Tomorrow's Saturday," Elin remembered. "And I'll be home, too."

As soon as Isä had washed and cleaned himself of the grime from the mine the next morning, they started. The streets were thronged with Saturday shoppers. The gay, many-coloured kerchiefs on the heads of the women fluttered through the crowds, like great butterflies among the tulips in Bell Park. And there was a trapper trudging across Elm Street complete with heavy knee boots, striped black and yellow jacket, and a huge pack on his back.

"Dobry den."

"Jako sa mas?"

Elin turned to stare at the two people chattering on the sidewalk. She drew closer to Isä. "Isä, listen."

Isä looked over at the men leaning their bulky bodies against a store front and waving their hands as they talked. "That is the language of Czechoslovakia, Elin.

That man work in mine with Isä. And see, over there, in front of big hardware store? There are some who speak language of Yugoslavia. That man in middle with bald head. He work in mine with Isä, too."

"Isä, would you say Finnish people are just as good as those people are?" Elin walked along quickly to keep up to Isä. "Just as good as people from Czechoslovakia and Yugoslavia and England?"

"It is not who is better than another, Elin." Isä guided her into the big bank building on the corner. "It is just that we all have to live together here in new land. All people are good."

Elin stood on tiptoe in the long line-up to read the sign at the end: "Savings Accounts." When their turn had come she looked up into the teller's cage. There was Wendy's father, peering down at her over his horn-rimmed spectacles, just like Wendy! Elin shoved the money towards him. "I want to put money in here," she said shyly.

Mr. Hill brushed his hand across his tiny black moustache. "You want to open an account, Miss?"

"That is right, an account, please," Isä nodded.

"Please sign here." Mr. Hill handed Elin several forms and she signed her name to them, the words running shakily downhill: "Elin Laukka." Then he gave her a little green book in a case.

"What's this for, Isä?" Elin turned it over to read the small print on the crest.

"That is bank book. Look inside. You will see the money is in there, all write down."

There it was, written in one of the columns. The money for the skating lessons had begun! Isä took her over to the high table in the middle of the room. He showed her how to sign the slip of red and white paper. "That is for you when you put money in," he explained. "Next time you do it all alone, and the next, and the next. You will know how."

They walked proudly out of the bank together.

One evening when Elin was getting ready to go home, Mr. Kurtsheff produced a bag from under the counter. Elin slipped out of the big white apron he had given her to keep her dresses clean, and watched him fill the bag with jellybeans and licorice. "Here. Little thing for Juhani," he said. "He don't get the candy much I guess, eh?"

"Oh, thanks, Mr. Kurtsheff! He'll love it. Would you mind if Isä and Äiti had some, too? We never have candy, only at Christmas sometimes."

Mr. Kurtsheff took another scoop of jellybeans and held it high above the open bag. The candy pattered into the brown paper like a sudden shower of hailstones, red, yellow, black, orange, white and green. "Mebbe that's better, not so? More to go round like. Vell, see you tomorrow same time, Elin."

Elin stood there silent for a moment. Then she leaned over the counter. "Mr. Kurtsheff, did you ever see anybody figure skate? Ever in your life?"

Mr. Kurtsheff pushed back his white cap and scratched the bald spot that shone like a skating rink on the top of his head. "I see all the kids skate on the lake sometimes, ven they play hockey."

Elin drew herself up with a pitying shake of her fair pigtails. "Oh, no, Mr. Kurtsheff! I mean figure skating. Like this." She spread out both her arms, clutching the bag of jellybeans in one hand, and lifted her leg as high as it would go. "It's like a bird, only prettier, and there's Mr. Crane down at the arena who teaches. Anna can figure skate. You know, Mr. Kurtsheff," she confided solemnly, "some day I'm going to be the best figure skater in the world."

"That's very nice," Mr. Kurtsheff agreed, not at all surprised. "Then we come to see you, Stepan and me. We cheer for you real loud."

Elin picked up the meat she was taking home for supper, and still clutching the bag of jellybeans, started for the door. "Well, goodnight, Mr. Kurtsheff. See you tomorrow. I have to go and get the mail."

"Goodnight, mine Elin!"

Now she had to hurry to reach the post office before it closed. The hands of the town clock said two minutes to six as she ran down Elm Street. She was all out of breath when she scurried up to the wicket. "Laukka, please!" she panted.

Two letters! One was the kind with a little window in it. A bill. Äiti wouldn't like that. The other was postmarked Finland and had Grandfather's stiff, upright handwriting on it. Äiti would be so happy to have a letter from home! Elin's feet skipped along the main street, over the pile of rocks beside the coal yard and down Finland Street.

"Know who this is from, Isä?" Elin waved the letter at him as he stood at the door, hands in his pockets, looking very sleepy. Isä was on the night shift. "You just get up, Isä? Where's Äiti?"

"Äiti is over with Mrs. Venna for the minute. And you are right, baby. Isä is just get up and he is tired still."

Elin stole in and laid the two parcels on the kitchen table. On top of the parcels she laid Grandfather's letter.

Surprise for Äiti, she thought, and went out to sit with Isä until Äiti found it. "The letter was from Grandfather," she confided in Isä's ear.

"That is good," he whispered back. "How you like to go for swim in lake after the supper, eh? If Äiti say we can go?" Isä still whispered secretly. "Just for a little swim till it get dark."

"Oh, could we, Isä?" Elin jumped up like a jack-in-the-box. "I could get the dishes wiped in a hurry and we . . . "

A loud shriek from Äiti made them both spin about like tops and rush into the house. Äiti was standing in front of the kitchen stove, waving the letter and shouting, "Isä! Isä! He's coming! He's coming to see us!" She rushed over to them, pointing to the second page of the letter, reading it aloud in Finnish to make them understand what she was saying. Slowly, she made herself read the exciting words. " 'I am getting old and it is not long I shall be here. And so, Miina, I have made up my mind to spend the little money I have saved on a trip to this Canada, to see you and your babies.' That's you and Juhani!" Äiti interrupted her reading to give Elin a swift hug. " 'I have been to the . . . boat man to see about my ticket,' " she went on with the letter. " 'And he tells me I can come in ten weeks' time.' " Äiti stopped reading and they all fell silent, dumbfounded by this news. Elin found it hard to follow the Finnish words. She tugged anxiously at Äiti's apron. "Grandfather's coming from Finland, Äiti? Is that what it says?"

Aiti dropped the letter to the floor and threw her arms around Isä's neck. They both began to talk at once, quickly and loudly.

"Isä's coming! Isä's coming!" Äiti swept across the

floor in a jig of happiness, her apron billowing round and round like a dancer's skirt.

Then she caught Elin's hands and they danced around the kitchen table. "Grandfather's coming from Suomi! Grandfather's coming from Suomi! Elin! Elin! Grandfather's coming!"

Elin shook herself free and looked up at Äiti dizzily. "Is it the Grandfather that used to skate who's coming to see us, Äiti? All the way from Finland?"

Äiti knelt beside her and hugged her close and Elin could feel Äiti's tears on her arm. "All the way from Finland, Elin. All the way from Suomi!"

6

The Accident

"Three more days and then summer holidays! Then just watch me throw this old thing away!" Anna swung her schoolbag back and forth, as if she would like to send it sailing over the shimmering rock hills.

"You'd better not," Elin cautioned. "School will be starting again in September and you'll need your books again."

"Not these. I'll pass into another grade and have to get a whole lot of new books. Anyway, who cares? It'll soon be summer holidays!"

"Three more days," Elin sighed, flinging her arm around Anna's shoulders. They strolled along through the heat of the June afternoon, down the dusty lane that led from the school to the main street and Mr. Kurtsheff's store.

"It seems as if it'll never go." Elin stopped to watch the awkward shunting of the freight train along the track down by the station. Smoke and soot poured from the engine. The glistening tracks stretched away to the far horizon in the afternoon sun, just like the holidays themselves, unfolding endlessly.

"Sulphur's bad today." Anna cleared her throat and

squinted up at the stacks of the Copper Cliff smelter with their rolling smoke plumes. "You know what my Pop told me?"

"No, what did he tell you?"

"That the smoke has never stopped pouring from the stacks at Copper Cliff for eighteen years!"

"Well, do you know what Isä told me?" Elin squared her shoulders with pride. "Isä says mines are just like the smoke at the smelter. They never stop going day or night. That's how they get enough nickel to send all over the world!"

"I guess my Pop knew that, too, but he never told me." Anna wrinkled her freckled nose in distaste at the strong smell of stale fried hamburgers trickling through an open restaurant door and joining hands with the heat. "Say, we're going to camp at the end of the week. It's sure going to be fun for two whole months. Where's your camp, anyway?"

"We haven't any camp." Elin kicked a little piece of rock slowly along in front of her with the scuffed toe of her boot. "Isä and I often go down to Bell Park to swim, and this year Äiti says we can take Juhani with us, maybe."

"Perhaps your Mom'd let you come and stay at our place for a while. Do you think she would? There's lots of room, and anyway, you could sleep with me out on the verandah. Do you think she would?"

"I could ask her." Elin's eyes sparkled. "Maybe she would. Is your place very far away?"

"Nope. It's just at the other end of Lake Ramsay, and Pop'll drive you out in the car. Say, when do you think you can come? You can stay for a week if your Mom'd let you."

A whole week at the lake with Anna! Beside Lake Ramsay, as blue as the Mediterranean Sea far across the ocean, so the teacher had said.

"I might even be able to come next week," Elin offered eagerly. "If Äiti will let me. What will we do at camp, Anna?"

"Oh, millions of things. We can go swimming all day. And there's a dock to dive off, too. Pop built it." Anna shivered at the thought of the cold water.

"Have you got a canoe?"

"We've got the prettiest red canoe on the lakeshore. Can you paddle, Elin?"

"No, but I'd love to learn. Would you teach me?" Elin shut her eyes and saw the little red canoe cutting through the water like the long red knife Mr. Kurtsheff used on the fat sausage rolls.

"Oh, sure. I've been paddling for years!" Anna shrugged her shoulders. "Mom'll let me take it out any time except after dark. But do you know what I like best about camp?"

"What?"

"We can stay up almost as late as we want to at nights and have fun."

"Maybe we could talk in bed, too." Elin was bursting with excitement. Imagine having somebody to talk to in bed!

They rounded another curve in the street and came in sight of Mr. Kurtsheff's store. Anna stopped short. "Golly, Elin. We forgot! You have to work for Mr. Kurtsheff this summer!"

"I forgot all about it!" Elin's castle of joy crumbled in a forlorn heap. "I won't be able to go to camp at all!"

"Maybe Mr. Kurtsheff will give you a little time off.

One Saturday or something. You just can't miss the fun at camp."

Elin set her mouth in a firm line. "Anna, I must get money for the lessons, whether I go to camp or not. It's so . . . "

"Elin! Elin!"

"Stepan's calling you!" Anna pointed down the street. "And look at him run!"

"Must be something important. Äiti says Stepan'd never run unless he had a stick of dynamite behind him."

"Look at his shirt-tail. Hey, Stepan!" Anna shouted. "Giddy, giddy gout! Your shirt's hanging out! That's what Wendy always says," she laughed.

"And his sock." Elin clucked her tongue disapprovingly, just like Äiti. "His sock's all rumpled down over his boot."

"Mr. Kurtsheff's coming out on his stoop. Stepan's stopping to talk to him."

"Let's hurry, Anna!" Elin grasped Anna's hand and they raced down the street, their eyes fixed upon Stepan and Mr. Kurtsheff. They saw Mr. Kurtsheff fling his hands up in the air and his cigar drop right out of his mouth. He was silent as they bounded up to him, and wiped his hands nervously up and down his dirty apron. Stepan kicked at the curb with his heavy black boots.

"Elin girl, you coming in mit your friend and having nice big ice cream, eh? Stepan boy, you, too, eh?" Mr. Kurtsheff examined the spots on his apron.

"Thank you very much, Mr. Kurtsheff, we'd love one." Mr. Kurtsheff must have had good news from Austria today. Maybe his daughter over there had had another baby. The last time that had happened he had given away, free, big slabs of Austrian sausage to the whole street!

"Gee, I'd love one, too, Mr. Kurtsheff. But I haven't any money with me today."

"That's no matter, Anna. You're heving ice cream cone just the same. So come in then." Mr. Kurtsheff lumbered up the steps ahead of them.

"I think I'd better go and see if I can help, Mr. Kurtsheff. They'll need men." Stepan stooped, pulled up his sock and started off down the street.

Go and help? Where was Stepan going to help that he would refuse a free ice cream cone? He must be sick or something. Sick! That was it! Something was wrong. Elin whirled around to Mr. Kurtsheff as he was lifting out the ice cream scoop, dripping sorrowfully in its basin of water.

"Something's wrong at the mine! Oh, Mr. Kurtsheff, has Isä been hurt?" Elin said.

Mr. Kurtsheff fumbled with the lid of the ice cream freezer and dropped the scoop on the floor. "It's mebbe nothing." He took such a long time to pick up the scoop that his face was red and wet. "The Stepan boy say things happen, but mebbe not so." He dug out a big, generous scoop of ice cream for Elin. But Elin was gone.

Her legs must run faster. They *must!* She would make them run as they had never run before! Past Mrs. Salo's! Isä was caught beneath a landslide of rock. Past Mrs. Haaki's! Remember the day Stepan's father had been brought home? He had never walked again. Past Mrs. Venna's! There were Mrs. Venna and Mrs. Koponen leaning over the front fence, staring out at her. She heard talking, Finnish words. "He is hurt bad, they tell me, Mrs. Koponen. Poor Mrs. Laukka!" Past

Mrs. Ronskainen's! And there was home.

A little black car was crouching fearfully in front of the house. Elin leaped up the steps two at a time. Äiti was sitting at the kitchen table, her head in her hands. Juhani tugged at her apron. Äiti looked up as Elin came in. "It's all right, little one. Take care of Juhani. He cry so much all day." Äiti was so quiet . . . but the bedroom door was closed and she was gazing anxiously toward it.

"Äiti, what's wrong?" Elin could feel the tears burn down her face. "Has Isä been hurt?" She collapsed in a sobbing heap beside Äiti. Juhani began to cry, too.

"It will be all right, little daughter." Äiti took Elin's head gently in her hands. "Doctor is there now. Isä will be all right." She stroked the blonde braids and said the words over and over, just like a lesson she might have learned at school. Then the bedroom door was opening and the doctor was tiptoeing out, his long white fingers holding a tiny gold watch. The frightening smell of ether and ointment walked out with him. But the doctor was smiling!

"He will be all right, Mrs. Laukka. His arms and legs are badly grazed and he has had a severe shock, but he will be all right." He smiled encouragingly at Äiti again and felt his little black bag to see if it were tightly closed. "He came to and spoke to me, and he does not suffer much. Don't worry now or I shall have two patients to look after."

"He is going to be all right?" Äiti unfolded herself as if standing up hurt her. "Nothing bad is wrong? He is going to be all right," she repeated, nodding her head to reassure herself.

"Yes, he'll have to take a few weeks off to heal up those grazes, and I've given him a pill or two to keep him asleep. But he'll be all right." He leaned over and patted Elin on the cheek. "And how are you today, young lady?"

"Fine, thank you," she said shyly. She felt her legs unwinding like the mechanical toy in Cochrane's Hardware Store. And there she was, standing in front of the doctor, carefully smoothing down her dress. "Can I please see Isä?"

"Not till tomorrow morning, young lady. Better let him get a good rest." The doctor was in a hurry to be off. His hat had a deep curve at the brim, just where his broad hand grasped it. When he put it on his head it perched there uncertainly as if to say, "Well, I don't expect to be here long so I won't hold on too tightly!" Then with a wink at Elin and a kindly smile at Äiti, he was gone.

Elin ran to the window to watch him clamber into the car. It whirled away up the dusty street. When she turned Äiti was standing still, her eyes bright with tears that hadn't come. Elin ran swiftly and hid her face in Äiti's apron.

7

Äiti Counts Her Money

"Poor Juhani's hot, isn't he? Never mind, we'll make him cool." Elin fanned him with an old Finnish newspaper. They sat together on the top verandah step.

"Hot! Hot!" echoed Juhani, hugging his old ragged teddy bear.

"Äiti always says July's the hottest month, anyway, Juhani. And maybe she'll let Isä and me take you paddling down to the lake. Would you like that? Paddle, Juhani? Paddle?" Elin wiped his sticky hands on her crumpled handkerchief.

"Pad! Pad!" Juhani flapped his arms uncertainly like a baby robin ready for his first flight. Teddy bear rolled down the steps with a soft thud.

Elin leaped to rescue him.

"Hi ya!" Anna appeared around the corner, looking very cheerful in a green sun suit and a crop of new freckles.

Anna! Elin waved excitedly. "Hello, Anna! I thought you were at camp!"

"We just came back for two days 'cause Mom had some shopping to do. But we're going back tomorrow." Anna flopped down beside them on the step. "Gee, you look white beside me! Have I ever got a sunburn!"

"Where've you been?" Elin jogged Juhani up and down between her knees so that he wouldn't cry.

"Just around to see Chrissie about coming to camp. Say, don't you think you could come this weekend? Even for Sunday? Elizabeth and Yolande and Chrissie's coming."

Elin shook her head, looking wistfully over the rocks in the direction of the lake. "I have to look after Juhani while Äiti takes care of Isä."

"Oh, golly, I almost forgot." Anna brushed her hair from her hot forehead. "I was supposed to ask how your Pop is getting along. Mom told me to."

"He's getting better all right. But he won't be going back to work for a long time. I heard the doctor telling Äiti."

"I wish you could come with us." Anna frowned. "Well, maybe you can come some other time. I guess I got to go home now for my supper." She ran off down the sidewalk. "Be seeing you!"

Elin watched her go. Dreams of a red canoe flashing through blue water, of brown bodies leaping in the sun, of silver birches under the stars, were running away with her. Anna would very likely be gone for the rest of the summer and wouldn't invite her again. She struggled to her feet, took Juhani in her arms and walked slowly into the house. "I have to peel potatoes for supper, Juhani. You sit there and be a good boy." She put him on the floor while she went to fetch the basket and the bowl.

"And why should I not go to work, Lemmin?" Äiti's voice lifted to a sudden peak of annoyance behind the closed bedroom door. "Mrs. Venna, she has a big family and she goes and makes money to help. Is there such a big reason why Mrs. Laukka must stay at home?"

"And what would your own Isä think when he comes from Finland, to see his daughter working hard to keep her family? He would think me a bad husband, not so? No, Miina, you stay home. We must give thanks that the mine pays the doctor bill and we have twenty dollars a week from the mine insurance since I am sick. We can make do with that."

"But what will happen when Isä comes from Suomi? I want to have nice fancy things for him and there is not enough money." Äiti's voice was almost crying. "And all the money for the tax bill and the coal bill. Where will we get that?"

Elin stood so quietly her throat made a little knot. Soon Äiti's laughter rang out again. Isä had a way with him to make everybody smile. But that night when Äiti sat darning socks by the kitchen table Elin noticed that the little line in her forehead was growing deeper and deeper. And her lips were all pursed up, like doing sums in her head while she darned. It was the same the next day, and the next.

One evening after Elin had come home from the store, Äiti was counting out a little pile of silver on the kitchen table. "Äiti," she asked, "do you and Isä have money in the bank, like me?"

Äiti paused in her counting and looked up at Elin. "We have some once, Elin. But now is gone. The bills must be paid, and Isä is not working so money is less." She sighed and scooped the glinting pieces of silver up in her broad palm. The little pickle jar, with splotches of white and green label clinging stubbornly to its glossy sides, rattled emptily as Äiti poured the money back into it. "I wish we have more," Äiti said gloomily. "It is sometimes hard to do with so little."

"I'm glad I have money in the bank, Äiti." Elin smiled importantly. "I have fifteen dollars now and that's a lot, isn't it?"

"A big lot," Äiti echoed. "Fifteen dollars pay maybe tax bill . . . or . . . pay maybe Mr. Kurtsheff for grocery, or . . ."

"But my fifteen dollars doesn't pay taxes or the grocery store, Äiti," Elin broke in. Äiti surely knew how important that fifteen dollars was. "Mine's for skating lessons, Äiti. You know that!"

"Yes, for the skating lesson, I know." Äiti's shoulders drooped a little wearily.

"I wish school would hurry and start so I can begin. If Mr. Crane will let me," Elin added doubtfully.

Äiti nodded.

Why does Äiti look at me so funny? Elin wondered. There was a sudden knocking at the door and she went to open it. There was Stepan.

"I came to tell you something," he grinned. "I'm going to dance in a concert. We just came home from Ukrainian Hall and they told us."

"What concert, Stepan?" Elin went out and they sat together on the top step.

"Mr. Ziniuk at the Hall, he teaches us Ukrainian dances after school, says we're all going to be in it." Stepan's face quivered with excitement. "It's a concert all about Sudbury and how it came to be."

"What do you mean, how it came to be?"

"Well, Mr. Ziniuk says a long time ago there wasn't any Sudbury at all. Just rocks and trees and lakes. Then somebody came and found nickel here and all sorts of people came here to live then."

"And you mean the concert is going to show how they came to Sudbury?"

"That's what Mr. Ziniuk says anyway, and it's going to have Yugoslavians and Czechoslovakians and Polish people in it, too. And even Bulgarians and Russians and Norwegians."

"Are there going to be any Finnish people in it, Stepan? There are all kinds of Finnish people in Sudbury."

"Yep, I guess so. I think Mr. Ziniuk said the Finnish people are going to do sort of exercises. Johnny Slobodi is going to play the mandolin." He gazed down at the dusty toes of his boots and sighed. "I wish I could play the mandolin. Dancing's kind of sissy stuff for big fellows like me."

"You're lucky you can even go and dance at the concert," Elin said. "I wish I could. When is it?"

"It's in two weeks and we got to work hard, Mr. Ziniuk says, so's we'll be the best ones there. It's going to be in the Capitol Theatre, right on the stage." Stepan stood up and began to walk slowly down the steps. "I got to go now, Elin. I got to tell Mom about it."

Elin ran after him and tugged at his arm. "Stepan, will it cost money to go and see it? The concert, I mean?"

"The tickets are a dollar and I have to sell some. I want to sell more than anybody else." Stepan groped in his pocket and drew out a dog-eared and dirty ticket. "Want to buy one, Elin?"

Elin gazed at him uncertainly. "I can't spend any money," she said finally. "I won't be going."

"Aw, you got money in the bank. You told me you had. Why don't you spend some of that?"

"I'm saving up for figure-skating lessons, Stepan,

like Anna takes. So I can't spend any money." The figures in the little green bank book danced across her mind. "I wish I could go, though."

"What do you want to take old figure-skating lessons for? That's sissy stuff. You ought to learn to play hockey instead." Stepan bounded away down the sidewalk. "Let me know if you want a ticket."

Elin walked thoughtfully into the house and into Isä's bedroom. He was sitting up reading the Finnish newspaper, his legs still bound with bandages. "And what is trouble that make my baby so sad?" he called. "You unhappy, Elin?"

Elin seated herself on the edge of the bed. "Isä," she began, "if you put money in the bank, is it all right to take it out again, please?"

"That is all depending what money will be used for, Elin. Now for something good, is all right to take money out." Isä folded the newspaper across his knees and looked over at her cheerfully.

"Oh, it's good all right, Isä. I know that. But when you want to do something else with the money that's good, too, it's hard to decide."

"Well, maybe if you do what you think is right thing at this time," Isä emphasized. "Maybe more money come for other good thing later. It is what is needed now that is important, little one."

Elin did not answer immediately and Isä leaned across the bed and took her hand in his. "Some time, Elin, is hard to give up the money, not so? But if you know it will help, then is not so hard, is it?"

"Oh, I'm not going to help anybody, Isä, except me, I guess." Elin's finger traced a giant fifteen on the faded coverlet. "I want to buy a ticket to the concert Stepan's going to dance in. It's going to be two weeks from now at the Capitol Theatre."

"That is for you to think, Elin." Isä leaned back on the pillows. He looked tired. "That is for you to think. Isä cannot help you." He smiled at her almost as if she were not there, and began to read his newspaper again.

Elin uncurled herself and slipped down from the bed. She walked slowly out to the kitchen. Something was wrong. Isä acted just as if he were forgiving her for something. Why? Had she said something she shouldn't have said?

Äiti was putting Juhani to bed and Elin could hear her murmuring softly to him in Finnish as she tucked in the covers. Äiti never sang any more now, only sometimes a sad, low tune, that sounded like Juhani's whimpering.

"Äiti," she said quickly, when her mother tiptoed out of the bedroom, "have I been a good girl?"

"Yes, Elin. You have been good." A smile played around Äiti's lips, the first smile Elin had seen there for a long time. "Now is there something Elin want, eh?"

"Does Isä think I'm good, too?"

"Miina! Miina! Come for a moment, please!" Isä called softly. Äiti bustled into the bedroom. Why did they whisper so softly? If she moved just a little closer to the bedroom door she might hear. But no! It wasn't right to listen to secrets. She must close her ears tight!

"Money in the bank," she heard Isä murmur. Then it must have something to do with money. Äiti and Isä were worried about money again. *I wish I was rich like Anna,* Elin thought. *I wish I had a whole lot of money, and then I'd give some of it to Äiti and Isä, and they wouldn't have to worry ever again.*

8

Stepan's Concert

"What was the concert like?" Elin ran to catch up to
Stepan as he ambled along the boardwalk, hands thrust
deep in his bulging trouser pockets. He was whistling but
there was no tune to it. "Was it good? Did you dance with
the other boys? What was it like?"

"It was real good, Elin. Mr. Ziniuk let us go and sit
in the front row and watch when our dance was done. We
watched the first part from the side of the stage. It was
real good."

"Well, tell me all about it." Elin danced along beside
him. "Who was in it?"

"Everybody was in it, and there was dancing and
singing." Stepan's eyes shone. "First of all, see, there
were two log cabins on the stage."

"Two log cabins! What were they?"

"That was what Sudbury was a long time ago. About
1860, I think the man said."

"What man said?"

"There was a man on the stage, and he was explaining
things from a long roll of paper he kept unfolding in his
hands. Anyway, the two log cabins used to be where the
city hall is now."

"You mean Sudbury was just two log cabins once? I don't believe it." Elin stared at him accusingly.

"That's what the man said. Two log cabins down by the creek. That was before the railway came and it was all a mistake that Sudbury came at all."

"All a mistake!" Elin was completely bewildered. "I didn't think cities came by mistake!"

"Sudbury did, anyway. It was when the Canadian Pacific Railway was starting to build a line through the North, the man said. A man named Ramsay came up here to find a way they could lay the railroad through and he got lost."

"Why, that's the name of the lake, Stepan. That's Ramsay." Elin looked surprised. "The same as the man's name."

"Sure, it was named after him. First of all it was called Lost Lake because they lost their trail. But then it was named after Mr. Ramsay. He camped right down where Bell Park is now, and do you know what?"

"No, what?"

"The axe Mr. Ramsay used to cut the trail through the woods right down in Bell Park, a long time ago, is still hanging in the City Hall." Stepan strutted along confident as a young rooster. "And did you know that Sudbury wasn't called Sudbury first of all? It was called St. Anne-of-the-Pines."

"Oh, what a pretty name! Who called it that?"

"Father Nolin, the first priest who came here. Nolin's Creek got its name from him, too."

"St. Anne-of-the-Pines." Elin tasted the words and loved them. "I wish it were called St. Anne-of-the-Pines now."

"It would have been, I guess, but a man whose name

was Mr. Worthington came along. He was a Justice of the Peace, and head man of a lot of things. He changed the name to Sudbury because his wife had been born in Sudbury 'way over in England." Stepan's keen eyes scanned the rock hills. "Anyway, there's hardly any pines left now. Forest fires burned them all up, roots and all. And do you remember teacher telling us how the sulphur from the Copper Cliff smelter killed all the green things, before they had the big chimneys built?"

"And did they have teachers and schools then, and everything?" Elin pushed Stepan down on the front steps of her house, so that he could finish the story of Sudbury.

"Sure. All the railway people came to lay the tracks and the children came with their moms and pops. They had an old log cabin for a school, that's all." Stepan dropped his elbows to his knees and buried his chin in his smudged hands. "I wish our school was a log cabin. That's where everybody used to meet and have square dancing to a fiddle and everything. What's square dancing, anyway, Elin?"

Elin pondered for a moment. "Teacher said once it's where people dance in squares, didn't she? It's like a folk dance of Canada, I think. People dance it in the country sometimes." She waited for him to go on.

"Then nickel and copper were found here, all because of another mistake."

"Another mistake! You mean somebody got lost again, Stepan?"

"Uh huh. A man by the name of Judge McNaughton. He got lost in the woods and the C.P.R. doctor took a search party out to look for him."

"Did they ever find him in the thick woods?" Elin looked worried.

"Sure. They found him sitting on a high rock right where Murray Mine is now. In the rock they saw copper shining and that's why they started to dig a mine there. Pretty soon they found nickel all around here, too. That's why Sudbury is a big city today. The man said so, anyway." Stepan paused for a deep breath. "And say, Elin, you know that shrine at the top of Nelson Street? The one where the Blessed Virgin is standing with all the rocks around her?"

"I know the one you mean. They used to put flowers there once, before all the rocks fell down."

"Well, that was built by a real count a long time ago, and do you know what? His wife was a real princess."

"Like what you read about in books, Stepan?"

"Yep, a real princess from Spain. And he was a Frenchman. Not like Yolande is French. He really came from France and lived right here in Sudbury and built the shrine."

Elin gazed at him with wide eyes. "I wish I could have gone to the concert and heard him say that. Was there anything else? What else did the man say? Who came next?"

"People came from all over the world as soon as the mines started, to work here. Some Polish people and English people and Ukrainians came from Southern Ontario. The play showed them getting off the train at the station. It was a funny train," Stepan grinned. "All made of cardboard. Gee, I think I'll be a train engineer when I grow up."

"How about the Finns? Finnish people came, too, didn't they?"

"Oh, sure, everybody. Finnish and Yugoslavians. Hungarians and Russians and Norwegians. Just everybody."

When Elin closed her eyes she could see them all, the Finns and the Slavs and the Hungarians and the Poles, all in their strange, many-coloured costumes. Just like the pictures in the movie she had seen one Saturday morning at the Public Library.

"First there was a lot of Finnish boys and they did exercises on the stage, to show how strong they were," Stepan remembered. "The man said they brought strength to Canada. Then there was an old Hungarian lady sewing on a blouse. It was all colours of the rainbow, with embroidery, too. There was a girl standing beside her with a Hungarian costume on and she was playing the violin, like the gypsies. The man said Hungarians brought beauty and colour and the gypsy heart to Canada."

"And were there more Ukrainians besides you?"

Stepan nodded proudly. "You bet. Some of our choir sang old Ukrainian folk songs. Johnny Slobodi played his mandolin, and me and the rest of the gang did our Ukrainian dances. And everybody clapped real loud."

"And what about the Russians? Did they do something?"

"A little Russian girl did a dance all dressed up in a short white skirt, and she danced on her toes. Kind of sissy stuff, but everybody clapped so loud she had to come back and do it again."

"Who come back and do it again, babies?" Äiti stood at the door with a plate of cookies. "Maybe we come to Finland Street now and have a cookie, eh?"

"Oh, Äiti! I've just been to the most wonderful concert, all about Sudbury and how it started." Elin helped herself to a large cookie and chewed on it, thoughtfully.

"To concert, Elin? How you go to concert when you

been at Mr. Kurtsheff's store with the work? And no money, too? How is that?"

"Golly, she saved a whole dollar, Mrs. Laukka!" Stepan started to chuckle but choked on cookie crumbs instead. "I was at the concert and I told her all about it. So now she knows what it was like, too. Honest, you'd never guess what Sudbury was like a long time ago."

"How did you come to Sudbury, Äiti?" Elin asked suddenly. "You and Isä?"

"Well, it is this way." Äiti looked a little sad, as if she were standing at a door opening slowly on a room full of good things that belonged to long ago. "Isä worked in factory in Helsinki. He see big notice in paper one day about miners needed in Canada. Big pay. Fine life. So we come. There is all."

"On a big boat over the ocean, Mrs. Laukka?" Stepan helped himself to another cookie.

"On great boat all the way. Äiti was sick sometimes but it soon all right. Then we come to big city Montreal. Many others come with us, people from Poland, Ukraine, Hungary, and other countries. We all get off boat and on train and ride all night long, sitting up straight. Oh, it is then I wish for my soft bed in Finland!" Äiti sighed, as if she could feel again the weariness of that first night in Canada. "But it is soon morning and the sun is shining so bright over a land all rock and lake. And we are in Sudbury!"

"Did everybody get off the train at Sudbury?" Elin brushed the crumbs from the wrinkled lap of her dress.

"Some do not get off with us. They go on to Winnipeg and prairie lands to be farmers. But Isä and Äiti have reach home, new home in Sudbury and north country."

"But the teacher told us in school, Äiti, that this isn't

really the north country any more."

"It is more north country when Isä and Äiti come, Elin. Sudbury is grow much since then, babies." Äiti squeezed her plump body in beside them on the step. "When we come it is more small. Not so many fine brick houses on the Hill. Not so many stores. More men from the woods on the streets. Now Sudbury grow big and fine city. It creep out between the rock hills like the legs of a long caterpillar that grow too big for the body."

"Well, I'm sort of glad it's like it is now," Elin sighed contentedly. "I wouldn't like to have lived here when it was real north."

"Gosh, I would!" Stepan leaped up. "I'd like to go real north now, where they have to fight bears and live in log cabins. Like Yellowknife maybe."

Äiti was bewildered. "This Yellowknife, it is north, too?"

"That's away up in the Northwest Territories and we study about it in school," Stepan explained. "I'm going up there one day. They've got bears and dog teams and everything. Gee, it's getting late." He squinted up at the sun hanging in the sky like a huge golden marble. "I gotta go home now and help Mom. G'bye, Elin! G'bye, Mrs. Laukka!"

Äiti watched him go, thoughtfully. "Stepan is maybe right," she murmured. "In the old days there is no worry about money. Maybe pay is not so good but we have money in the bank then."

Elin followed her slowly into the house. *But I have money in the bank now!* she thought joyfully. *A lot of money!*

9

The Music Festival at Last

"Äiti, how many more weeks till Grandfather comes from Finland, please?" Elin wiped the last green and yellow supper dish carefully, and put it away in the cupboard. "Will it be very long now?"

"Now is August. Grandfather come in last week of October month." Äiti folded up a bill and dropped it into the glossy little pickle jar. "Äiti count. One . . . two . . . three . . . " She pursed up her lips and counted silently, her head nodding for every figure. "Eight weeks till my Isä come from Suomi. But then there is also Music Festival before that. Remember?"

"Maybe I won't be able to go to the Music Festival this year, Äiti." Elin slammed the cupboard door shut. "Maybe Mr. Kurtsheff won't let me off for the day."

"Not go to Finnish Music Festival at Trout Lake? You never miss, ever since you little girl, Elin. Every year is Finnish Music Festival at Trout Lake. All Finns go to that."

"I know, but Saturday is the busiest day at the store and Mr. Kurtsheff needs me, Äiti. If I leave him maybe he won't let me work any more. And I just have to have the money!"

"You got much money now, Elin? You almost rich girl?"

"Lots of money, Äiti." Elin flourished the little green bank book in front of Äiti.

"You soon wear that book all out, you read it so much," Äiti smiled.

"Yes, but even if it does wear out, Isä says I can't have a new one till this one's all filled up. And look!" Elin opened the bank book for Äiti to see. "It's not nearly filled up yet!"

"Yes, but there is lots of figures there." Äiti traced down the long rows of numbers with her blunt finger. "You rich girl, Elin."

"Who is this rich girl? Who is she? I need to find rich girl." Isä limped in from the backyard, his hands in his pockets.

"It's me, Isä," Elin called. "I'm rich. Look! In my bank book!"

"There is lucky girl who is rich and have no bill to pay." Isä poked Elin playfully in the ribs and looked over her head at Äiti.

But Äiti was looking hard at the little green bank book. "That money would pay much bill, Lemmin, eh?"

"It's going to pay a skating bill, Äiti, isn't it?" Elin smiled up at them both. "That's what it's for, a skating bill! See! I have a bill to pay just like you and Isä."

"It is good to have the bill that is not yet made," Isä said. "That is good."

"Isä, do you think I should ask Mr. Kurtsheff to let me off on Saturday for the Music Festival?"

"Oh, yes. My Elin never miss Music Festival. There is no harm to ask."

On the Tuesday before the Music Festival, Elin was

fanning herself with an old paper plate at Mr. Kurtsheff's counter. "Mr. Kurtsheff, do you like to have fun?" she queried. He was washing off the meat shelf, his heavy red cheeks quivering with the exertion.

He paused and held the grey cloth suspended in mid-air, limp as an old rag doll. "Vell, yes. I'm liking the fun, too," he remembered solemnly. "Ven I'm little boy I'm having all kinds tricks I'm playing on peoples, and mine Mama is giving me always the spanking."

"But you're not a little boy now, Mr. Kurtsheff," Elin laughed. "And you're always playing tricks on me!"

"Sure! Now I'm still liking the fun and I'm not having the spanking, not so?" He chuckled so heartily at his joke that his apron shook. "Vy is you asking me that question, please?"

"Well, you see, Mr. Kurtsheff . . . " Elin hesitated, trying to think of the best words. "Well, I wonder if I could have Saturday off to have some, please." She waved the paper plate very quickly in front of her face.

"Some vat?"

"Fun, Mr. Kurtsheff! Fun! That's what we've been talking about." Then she saw Mr. Kurtsheff's wink at the ice cream freezer. "Oh, Mr. Kurtsheff! You knew all the time!"

Mr. Kurtsheff laid the rag down on the counter and eased himself on to the high stool with a big sigh. "So, already you're getting little tired of working here mit your friend, mebbe? You're wanting to go play mit the other girls."

"Oh, no, Mr. Kurtsheff!" Elin frowned, leaning over to him eagerly. "I just love it here. Honest I do. I wouldn't ever like to go. Why, I'll even be sorry when school starts and I can't stay here any more."

"Then vat is this wanting the fun for, please?"

"It's the Music Festival at Trout Lake I want to go to, please. Remember? We had it last year, too, and the last year before that, and the last year before that, and the last year . . . "

"Mine goodness! Wait a minute there!" interrupted Mr. Kurtsheff, with a broad, pleasant smile. "You back up so fast I'm not keeping up mit you. Yes." He took out his red dotted handkerchief and mopped his face. "Yes, I'm remembering that Music Festival. Music Festivals is lovely things. Mine Vienna now, that is the place for the music. Ah, it is always the music and the violin in every little square in the city, and in the beergartens. All the life is just one big Music Festival in mine Vienna." He was silent again, and Elin waited anxiously. She did not dare to interrupt his dreaming, for she knew he was once again in his "old country" with the sound of the violin in his ears and the waltz in his heart.

A little old lady shuffled in. "One pound of round steak minced, please," she piped. Mr. Kurtsheff lumbered off to wait on her. When she had gone he turned to Elin again. "So, you're wanting the fun, eh, Elin girl? Vell, I'm thinking mebbe you go to your music and the boss he will try to get along okay for one day."

"Oh, Mr. Kurtsheff, I'm so glad," Elin beamed. "I'll work twice as hard on Monday to make up for it!"

"Ho, ho! But there ain't the business on Monday same as Saturday. How you work that, eh?"

"Well . . . " Elin considered. "Well, I'll tell Stepan and all the rest to save their nickels for ice cream cones till Monday, instead of spending them after the movies Saturday!"

"Tell them to spend the nickel both days," the fat

storekeeper chuckled. "Is better for Kurtsheff all round!"

Now the weather just had to be fine! Elin was going to the Music Festival! Tuesday night was clear and shiny with stars. Wednesday morning was sparkling with sunshine. Wednesday night hung heavy with clouds! Thursday it rained, a lively rain that hummed as it fell. The thousands of drops hissed against the window of Mr. Kurtsheff's store . . . *Fine day . . . Maybe! . . . Fine day . . . Maybe!* Friday morning the rock hills still glistened grey and wet, but the sun was trying to see his golden face in them. The rain was over.

Friday night after supper Elin went outside to look up at the sky for clouds. *The stacks of the smelter look just like a ship tonight,* she thought. *Like the big ship Grandfather will be coming on from Finland. Sailing right across the sky with the smoke flying.*

Stepan sauntered round the corner as she stood on the front walk. "What's the matter, Elin?" he asked. "See an airplane somewheres?"

"I'm looking for rain, that's all."

"What for?" Stepan eyed her with curiosity.

"'Cause I don't want rain, that's why."

"Well, for goodness sakes! If you don't want rain, why are you looking for it?"

"I'm trying to find out if it's going to rain, that's all. How can you tell, anyway, Stepan?"

"Gee, I dunno. It comes from clouds, doesn't it? And there's no clouds there, is there?"

Elin pointed to faint traces of clouds. "Do you suppose rain could come from them? Wouldn't it be awful if it rained tomorrow?"

"I don't see why it'd be so awful." Stepan sat on the edge of the sidewalk, his chin in his hands. "It's gotta rain some time, hasn't it?"

Elin brushed off the boards and sat down beside him. "Stepan, it just can't rain tomorrow, on account of our Music Festival at Trout Lake. Remember?"

"Gee, you must have fun at that festival. I wisht I was a Finnish boy so's I could go, too. I gotta cut Graham's lawn tomorrow. Maybe if I cut it real good, he'll give me seventy-five cents."

Elin sat quietly watching an ant with a tiny load struggle across her shoe. Then she smiled. "Say, Stepan, why don't you come to the Festival with us tomorrow? I don't see why you couldn't. Nobody said a Ukrainian boy couldn't come anyway. Wait a minute, I'll go and ask Äiti." She jumped up as she spoke and ran into the house. "Äiti says it'll be all right," she called out. "You can come in the truck with us. Do you think your Mom'll let you?"

"Gee, I can ask her." Then Stepan frowned. "Will there be boys there? I don't want to go if it's just a lot of girls."

"Oh, lots of boys, Stepan." Elin settled herself on the step again. "Some older than you, too."

"What am I gonna do about Graham's lawn though? If I don't cut it tomorrow I betcha he won't ever let me cut it again."

"That's easy," Elin explained. "Get up early and cut it before we go. The truck doesn't leave till after one o'clock. Go and ask your Mom."

Elin sat waiting for his return, winding her pigtails about her fingers and watching a lone crow wing over the rocks.

"Mom says I can go!" Stepan whooped breathlessly, as he raced back up Finland Street. "If it doesn't cost anything I can go!"

66

"It doesn't cost anything for you, anyway." Elin looked as pleased as Stepan. "C'mon and play 'I Spy'."

Elin opened her eyes the next morning and looked around the cracked walls of her bedroom as she always did. "There's no sun!" she shouted, leaping out of bed and running to the window. Grey clouds covered the sky. Elin's heart sank at the sight of them. She dressed quickly and flew downstairs. There was Äiti already cutting thick slices from the loaf and spreading them with butter.

"Äiti, there's no sun!" she cried. "Do you think it will rain?"

"Äiti is get the lunch for the Music Festival, so it better not to rain!" Äiti flourished the bread knife warningly at the grey clouds pressing in at the window.

Elin ran out after breakfast. "Äiti! Äiti!" she shouted, racing back to the kitchen. "There's a little bit of blue. Just a little bit!"

"Blue? Blue?" Juhani questioned his teddy bear on the floor.

"Blue, Juhani!" Elin bent down to give him a squeeze. "Maybe it'll be fine after all!"

Stepan came running up the walk at twelve o'clock, wet grass plastered on his boots and pant legs. "You're early, Stepan," Elin called, one arm hugging the verandah post.

"I know," Stepan grinned apologetically. "But I finished Graham's lawn early and I didn't want to be late!"

"Look!" Elin pointed to the sky. "There's enough blue to make a Dutchman a pair of breeches!"

"Half a dozen Dutchmen," Stepan corrected. "It's going to be a swell day, I bet."

"Time to go! Time to go!" Äiti finished tying the string around the last package of lunch.

"The truck is wait for us at the end of Finland Street!" Isä shooed Elin and Stepan out of the door and took Juhani on his shoulder.

"Stepan! The sun's shining!" Elin raced along in front of him.

"Beat you to the end of the street, Elin!" Stepan boasted.

It was exciting, clinging to the sides of the truck, feeling the wind rush over their faces as they went skimming by the great mounds of rock along the highway.

"Danger! Go slow!" Stepan read a big yellow sign standing on the roadside.

"We're not going very slow!" Elin called. "Oh, look! There's Trout Lake, Stepan!"

"C'mon, Elin! There's a sailboat 'way out there. Let's watch it." They jumped down from the truck and ran to the rocks at the edge of the lake. Far out a little red sailboat hung suspended between sky and island.

"Don't fall in the water!" Äiti warned. "I go to club-house to take food." She struggled with her arms full of parcels to the little house nestled in a mound of stone. Excited Finnish chatter and laughter drifted through the windows.

"What's in that funny old shed over there?" Stepan pointed his stubby finger toward an old grey wooden building crouched on another heap of rock.

"That's the steam bath, Stepan. Haven't you ever seen a steam bath?"

"Nope. What's a steam bath?"

"Well, it's a lot of rocks and the men make them very

hot with a big fire. Then they pour cold water over them and it gets all steamy. Whoever wants a steam bath goes and lies in there on a shelf and then they go and jump in the lake. It makes you feel tingly all over."

"Look!" Stepan pointed to the little hut on the rocks. "There's your Mom, and she's coming out again with all the other ladies."

"They just went to put the food in till supper time. Shh, Stepan! Don't talk any more. The man's going to speak." She looked up at a high rock where a short, fat man began to welcome them with a speech of melodious Finnish.

"What's he saying, Elin?"

"He says he hopes everybody has a good time and he's glad we've come."

She listened quietly for a moment and then she jumped up. "Come on, Stepan," she called. "He says the races are going to start on the grass near the hut." She grabbed Stepan's hand in hers and they ran to the green grass beyond the rock. "You wait here while I run, Stepan," she cautioned as she ran into line. "There's three races I can go in, so yell for me, will you?"

"I'll yell real hard." His eyes followed her to the starting point. He cheered loudly as the race began, but only in the last race of all did she come first.

"What did you get, Elin?" he asked, as she came running over to him.

"A little comb in a tiny blue case, and it's got Finland Forever written right across it. Oh, just wait till I show Anna tomorrow."

"Maybe I could go in the race for the boys as big as me. Do you suppose it'd be all right?"

"My goodness, yes. Anybody can go in as long as

they're not big people like Äiti and Isä, and they even have races for them, too, after. Listen! There's a man calling boys ten to twelve. Now go on, Stepan!"

Elin stood where she could see him. "Come on, Stepan! Run hard!" she shouted as the man gave the signal to go.

Stepan was first all the way but, just as his foot crossed the finish line, he slipped and fell headlong against the rope. Elin ran to help him to his feet. A little knot of people gathered around him.

"Oh, Stepan, you grazed your knee. Here, I'll do it up with my hankie."

"Aw, let it alone, Elin," he objected huffily, his face all red. "Gosh, I'm no sissy."

The man in charge of the races came up and examined Stepan's knee. "It will be all right," he advised. "Not much hurt. Here is for fine boy." He patted Stepan on the shoulder and handed him a small parcel wrapped in white tissue paper. "Maybe that help to take the hurt away for you."

Stepan tore it open in great excitement. There, in the folds of the crisp wrappings, was a shining pocket knife.

"Gee, wait till I show Mom." Stepan's face beamed. "I always wished I had a pocket knife. Gee . . . " He fondled it lovingly with his grubby hands.

"Now don't cut yourself, Stepan." Elin pulled him over to the side of the grass. "Here come the boys to do their tumbling exercises. Let's watch from here."

Stepan's eyes were wide with approval as the supple young bodies twisted and turned in formation on the grass. "Gee, I bet I could do that! It looks like fun."

"Here come the girls now," Elin whispered. "Look, over there, in Finnish folk costume."

"Is that Finnish folk costume? It's almost as nice as Ukrainian, isn't it?" Stepan watched the girls as they wove in and out, clapping their hands and singing together.

"I like the way they sing as they dance. Maybe I'll be able to do it one day, when I get older. It's something like figure skating."

Stepan tilted his nose in the direction of the little house on the rocks and sniffed hungrily. "I smell something good Elin. Is it nearly time to eat?"

"I saw Äiti and all the ladies go in a while ago. So I guess it's almost ready."

Stepan rolled his eyes and rubbed his stomach. "I'm hungry as anything. What will we be having to eat?"

Elin tried to remember what she had seen Äiti put in the basket. "Well, there's mojakkaa," she began slowly.

"What's that?"

"Mojakkaa is a thick soup with potatoes and all sorts of vegetables in it. They make it in Finland, too. Äiti told me."

"What else?" Stepan was getting hungrier every minute.

"Then there'll be fresh salted salmon made into sandwiches with rye bread."

"You mean the salmon isn't cooked?"

"Oh, no, it's not cooked. But you'll love it." Elin paused to consider. "Then there's always coffee and coffee bread and all sorts of cakes and cookies like they make in Finland."

Stepan was dubious. "How do they know how to make them here if they make them in Finland?"

"'Cause Äiti learned when she was a little girl in Finland, that's why, silly. Same as your Mom makes

Ukrainian things for you. But come on, Stepan. They're beginning to line up at the door." She grabbed his arm and they hurried to join the queue at the door of the little cabin.

"Let's go over and eat on the rocks," Elin suggested. They flopped down at the edge of the water and began to eat with great gusto.

"I wish I owned one of those islands," Stepan mumbled, his mouth full of salmon and rye bread. "Maybe I will one day. I'll build a cabin on it, too."

Elin brushed the crumbs from her lap and sipped her coffee. She gazed over the shimmering water to the tiny islands of rock and birch tree that dotted the lake. "It would be nice," she sighed. "Anna has a camp on the other side of the lake."

"Gee, I'm so full I couldn't even eat a blueberry." Stepan looked out over the green shiny shrubs growing close to the rolling rocks. "There's lots this year, too. Mom wants me to pick her some."

"Maybe I'll come and pick, too. Then Äiti can make a blueberry pie."

"Oh, I'll be going with the gang from the Donovan, I guess." Stepan gave her a sudden poke in the arm. "Hey, Elin," he whispered. "What are all those people going to do, and the little, fat man? See? Over there in the trees?"

Elin put her finger to her lips. "Shh, Stepan! That's the choir and they're going to sing. That's where they always stand, up there on the rock under the birch and pine trees. Shh! They're going to begin."

Softly, so softly that the folk seated on the ground could scarcely hear, the choir began to sing. It was a song of Finland, "Oi Kallis Suomenma," a song of the dear Finnish homeland, and in the quiet of the evening the notes rose and swelled in a mighty rush of sound. And in this song, they wove for the Finnish people at their feet a spell of the greatness and the beauty that was the Finland they knew, the sapphire lakes with their emerald islands, the shores of stalwart spruce and graceful birch, and the vast forests of the old land. They sang of the wheat fields, glistening like the bronze shields of the mighty in the summer sun, and they sang until the sun slipped softly down over the edge of the world.

In time with the flow wash of the water on the rocks, the choir began the gentle notes of its last song: "Finlandia, Oi synnyinmaa oot mulle äiti armain; Dear land of home, our hearts to thee are holden."

Elin's throat tightened as the voices soared above the tree-tops. She looked over at Stepan. He was trying to pry open his new pocket knife with his stubby fingers.

10

Farewell to Skating

"Anna, do you know what the sulphur looks like today?" Elin paused on top of the hill. Sudbury City lay below them, wrapped in a gown of sulphur smoke drifting from the Copper Cliff smelter with the west wind.

"No, what?"

"Just like the yellow shawl Theresa wore at the Hallowe'en masquerade party, when she was all dressed up like the Hungarian gypsy. And the sun's the gypsy campfire."

"It doesn't look like gypsies to me," Anna snorted. "It's just old sulphur and it hurts my throat so that I can hardly breathe." She coughed and wrinkled her nose. "Say, Elin, skating starts next week. Have you got enough money for the lessons?"

"I think I'll have enough." They sauntered along in the warmth of the September day. "I haven't even spent a nickel of the money I earned. But now school's started Äiti says I better not work at the store any more."

"I'd love it if you could take. Of course, you'll only be in beginner's class at first, but if you're good, Mr. Crane will move you up. Perhaps even with us."

"Anna, remember what Wendy said? Maybe Mr.

Crane won't let me take lessons. Maybe he won't like me 'cause I live on Finland Street."

"Oh, that old Wendy's always talking," Anna laughed.

A big blue bus honked behind them and rattled to a stop. Three men with tin lunchpails clambered down and hunched up the laneway home.

"There goes the shift from the mine. It must be nearly four o'clock. Is your Pop back at work yet?"

"He went back two weeks ago," Elin nodded. "He's all better now. I'm glad, too."

They came to the corner of Finland Street and Elin started up the boardwalk. "You coming to see Mr. Crane when we register next week then, Elin?" Anna called after her.

"I'm coming, so you tell me the day. I want to put on my best green dress."

It was Thursday after school when she and Anna went to the arena. Elin smoothed her green dress neatly about her and patted her pigtails into place. *Perhaps if I look nice and smile,* she thought, *Mr. Crane won't mind if I live on Finland Street.* Elin smiled fearfully.

A small crowd was gathered at one end of the rink where a table was set up. Elin could see Mr. Crane sitting behind the table, with a big book in front of him.

"You have to go and sign your name," Anna explained. "And then he puts you in your class. He's nice, though. So don't be scared."

"Hurry up, Elin! Get in line!" Wendy shouted across the ice. Elin waved to her. Then she felt the small pocket below the belt of her dress. Yes, the bank book was still there where she had put it before leaving home. She could show Mr. Crane she had enough money to take lessons.

"What are those big girls whispering about in the corner," she wondered. "They're looking at me."

There was a loud giggle. Elin felt hot all over. "They're laughing at me because I live on Finland Street!"

"Go on, Elin!" Anna gave her a sudden shove with her firm, plump little body. "What's the matter? Go and get into the line before it's too late."

"What if Mr. Crane says I can't, Anna?" Elin held her head down to hide her tears. "That's what Wendy said. Because I live on Finland Street."

"Oh, Elin, it's not true!" Anna glared like an angry kitten. "Anyway, Wendy never said that exactly. She said nobody from Finland Street had ever taken lessons before. Come on! Please!" She caught Elin's arm and pulled her into the line that straggled like an idle skipping rope up to Mr. Crane's desk.

Maybe it would be all right then, if Anna thought so. Another loud giggle bubbled from the corner. Elin turned quickly and hurried back across the ice, stumbling through the dark. Hot tears burned her face.

"Hey, Mr. Crane, you better sign up Elin Laukka! She's going away without signing!" Wendy's voice rang out behind her.

"Elin! Elin Laukka! Wait one moment, please!" Mr. Crane was running across the ice towards her! Where could she hide? He knew now that she, Elin Laukka of Finland Street, had dared to come for lessons. He was going to punish her because she lived on Finland Street!

She spied an empty space under the seats and started toward it. It was too late. There was Mr. Crane! He caught her hand in his.

"Now what's the matter, Elin?" He did not sound angry! He was frowning but it wasn't a cross frown. "Your name is Elin Laukka, isn't it?"

Elin choked, her throat too thick to answer.

"Then come back up here with me and tell me what the trouble is. Your little friend Wendy told me you were running away. What's up? You never learn anything by running away from things, you know."

"I live on Finland Street, and Isä is poor, and I know lessons are for people who don't come from Finland. Anyway, I'm going home ..." She wiped her face on her sleeve. "I wanted to take skating so bad. But I don't care now." Mr. Crane looked down at her, bewildered. Then he put his arm gently around her shoulders. "Elin, why should I not like you because you live on Finland Street? I think Finns are some of the finest folks in Sudbury. And Finland is such a beautiful land. I remember every minute I spent there."

"You've been to Finland? To the Finland Isä and Äiti came from?" Elin was astounded. "Then you must know my *grandfather!*"

"Well, there are a great many grandfathers in Finland, Elin," Mr. Crane smiled. "Maybe as many as there are in Canada, so I'm afraid I don't know *your* grandfather. I went to Finland when I was a very young man, studying skating in Europe."

"But you must have seen Grandfather, then," Elin insisted. "My grandfather won the skating prize in Helsinki. He was the best figure skater there. Äiti told me!"

Mr. Crane's mouth formed a surprised O, and he placed his hands on Elin's shoulders and looked keenly into her eyes. "Your grandfather used to be a figure skater, Elin? He won prizes at Helsinki?"

Elin nodded.

"Well, well, indeed," he breathed softly. "That would be before my time. But now you have come to follow in Grandfather's footsteps. Is that right?"

"Maybe I won't be famous," Elin murmured. "But I can try. Even if we are poor, I can try."

"What difference does it make if you are poor?" Mr. Crane frowned again. "Why, I'm none too rich myself," he chuckled. "Never have been. When I was a young man, a student of figure skating, there was always something I had to give up so I could go on with my skating lessons. There were even times in Europe when I was hungry because there weren't enough pennies in my pocket to buy a proper meal. Did you know," he added softly, "that some of the world's greatest men and women were poor when they were small like you? Yes, even poorer than you."

"Were they?" Elin's blue eyes looked at him, unbelieving.

"Indeed they were, and it was being poor that helped them. After all, being famous is having people love what you do and what you are, not what you have. Now tell me, who told you I didn't like Finnish people or poor people?"

Elin shook her head and was silent. Mr. Crane asked another question. "And have you money of your own, Elin, that you can use for taking lessons?"

"I worked at Mr. Kurtsheff's store all summer and saved up." Elin fumbled for the bank book to show him. "Is that enough for lessons?" She looked up at him eagerly, her tears almost gone.

"Plenty," Mr. Crane answered. "But come with me. We have things to say to these young people." He took her hand again and they walked up to the table. He had no need to call for quiet. Silence had crept like a stranger among the boys and girls.

Mr. Crane looked at them for a moment. "Boys and girls," he began. "Before any more of you register with me for the winter skating season, there are a few words I want to say to all of you." He took them all in with a keen, penetrating glance. "Here in Northern Ontario, perhaps more than in any other part of Canada, the races of the world are gathered from all the far away and exciting ends of the earth. How many of your mothers and fathers came from other lands?"

"Mine, Mr. Crane, mine came from Poland, Mom, and Pop, too!" That was Anna.

"And mine, sir, mine came from Hungary!"

"My father's from Croatia!"

"My mother's Italian!"

The shouts rang out from dozens of voices across the arena.

"Me, too! My grandfather was King of Ireland!" It was Wendy elbowing her way to the front. A roar of laughter followed. Even Mr. Crane smiled.

It's funny, Elin thought as she laughed along with the rest. *Wendy doesn't mind at all when people laugh at her. She laughs, too. But I'd feel just terrible if they laughed at me!*

But Mr. Crane was speaking again. "Yes, from Ireland and everywhere they came, because they wanted to make their homes in Kapuskasing, in Timmins, in Cochrane, in North Bay, and even in Sudbury, our own city." He paused to clear his throat. "Had it not been for these good people who travelled courageously across the seas, Canada would perhaps have no gold mines, no coal mines . . . yes, and no nickel mines, because there would have been no one strong and brave enough to work in the darkness beneath the earth. Now, can you see what that would mean to all of us?"

"I guess that means there just wouldn't have been any Sudbury at all, if it hadn't been for the New Canadians. I guess they're more important than anybody!" Elin knew that voice. It was Wendy Hill's!

"That's right, Wendy," Mr. Crane nodded approvingly. "And thank you for being plucky enough to speak up. But there's something else." Elin saw Mr. Crane's mouth set in a firm line. "In Sudbury there are no longer New Canadians. Every one of you, whether you're English, Irish," he winked at Wendy, "Czechoslovakian, Hungarian, Polish, or Finnish," he smiled down at Elin, "every one of you, no matter from what far away country your people have come, is a citizen of Canada, with a fair right to take part in all our Dominion has to offer." He leaned forward across the table to give his words emphasis. "Remember that not so long ago, all our mothers and fathers, or great-grandmothers and great-grandfathers, were New Canadians. They all came from the old lands to pioneer in this new one, English and French as well as others. Do you understand that?"

There was a subdued murmur. "Yes, Mr. Crane. Yes, sir."

"Perhaps this year we can find some way in our Carnival to help you see what I mean." He sat down suddenly. "That will be all. Next, please. Oh, it's you, Elin!"

Elin took the pen in her hand and signed her name shakily. "Will I be able to go in the Carnival, too?" she whispered.

"Of course you will," Mr. Crane promised. "If you try hard and do as I say."

When Elin came running into the house on Finland Street she stared around in surprise. The kitchen was deserted. It was Isä's week for night shift, so she knew he, as well as Äiti, should be home. Then she heard voices from the bedroom. She crept to the foot of the stairs. She would steal up and surprise them.

Her foot was on the first step when she stopped short in astonishment. Äiti was crying! Why, Äiti never cried, except when she was very happy. But this was not happy crying. These were great, deep sobs that Elin knew well, for she often felt them herself. She listened. Isä was murmuring soft Finnish words. "We shall manage, Miina. Something will turn up. Never yet have we not had enough. Perhaps your Isä will bring some with him when he comes."

Elin crouched on the stair. What was the matter? What was Grandfather going to bring with him from Finland that would make them all happy again?

"It is no use, Lemmin. It is the tax bill. If we do not pay the tax bill there will be no house to live in. Then what happens to my Isä who comes to see us from Suomi?" Äiti burst into a fresh torrent of weeping. Elin crept quickly away from the stairs and went outside to the front steps. So that's what it was. The money again. There was no money in the pickle jar to pay the tax bill.

Elin sat biting her lip. She watched the pale September haze over the rock hills. Then, slowly, thoughtfully, she drew the little green bank book from her pocket. She opened it at the last entry. A lot of money. Perhaps it would pay the tax bill. She suddenly knew why Isä had looked upon her with disappointment. She knew now why Äiti had gazed at her so hopefully every time she mentioned the bank account. *I really knew all the time,* Elin thought. *They hoped I would help them!*

She sprang to her feet and up the stairs. "Everything'll be all right, Äiti. Honest it will. Here! It's all yours to pay the bill. I don't want it. I signed up but that's all right. Mr. Crane will let me off." Elin was talking loudly and quickly, trying to hide the disappointment in her face.

"You give us the money, Elin?" Äiti's face shone through her tears. "You do not want to take the lesson?" Isä could not speak. He just looked at her and his eyes shone with pride.

"I can take some other time," Elin declared stoutly. "Maybe next year I can work for Mr. Kurtsheff and take. I'll be one year older then, too, and I can learn even better, maybe. Anyway, here's the money. You can take it out of the bank any time."

Äiti stared unbelievingly at the figures in the bank book. Isä opened his arms and Elin ran into them, hiding her face on his shoulder. He felt her warm tears brushing his arm. "My fine little Elin," he murmured. "She is good girl and brave girl." He stroked her hair with his rough hand.

"Isä," Elin turned her face up to his. "What are taxes, anyway?"

"Taxes?" Isä searched for an answer. "Taxes . . ."

"Taxes is taxes," Äiti declared gloomily, still fingering the little green bank book. "Taxes is just something you have to pay."

11

All the Way from Finland

"It wasn't as hard as I thought it would be, Äiti. Giving up the money, I mean." Elin sat curled up in her favourite chair by the kitchen window.

"Äiti and Isä is very proud of Elin for being such good girl and sign the cheque for to pay the taxes."

"Anyway, I learned something, Äiti. How to sign a cheque." Elin remembered the funny feeling inside her, the day she wrote her name on the cheque for Isä. "Now I know almost everything about banks, I guess. That's important."

"Never mind, baby. The days fly by and Grandfather come soon." Äiti made her needle fly, too, as she put a neat darn in the heel of Isä's grey sock. "Now is September late and the hills in this month make me think of beautiful piece of cloth we weave at home in Finland, with the soft colour of brown and grey, orange and red, all weave together very fine."

"Oh, Äiti!" Elin jumped up to count the weeks on the calendar. "Maybe Grandfather's on his way from Finland right this minute. How long is it now?"

"We wait, little one." Äiti patted Elin's head. "We wait and see."

"And then after Grandfather comes it won't be long till Christmas! Äiti, it's wonderful having so many things to wait for!"

The waiting was not long. The very next day, when Elin came racing home from school, Äiti was out on the verandah waving a letter. "It is come, Elin!" she cried. "From my Isä!"

"Is he on his way, Äiti?" Elin was up the steps in one bound. "Really on his way?"

"He is come and will be here soon, he say, Elin. Oh, little one, Äiti is so happy!"

"I'll be glad when he gets here." Elin followed Äiti into the kitchen, and poked her books into a corner on the kitchen shelf. "I can't work in school any more 'cause all the time I think about Grandfather."

"But you must work hard at school, Elin baby, to show Grandfather what smart girl you are."

"Grandfather! Grandfather! That is all the word I hear! Always Grandfather!" Elin tried to sound like Äiti as she pulled the tablecloth from the drawer.

"So, you make the fun of old Äiti, eh?" Äiti bent to give her a playful spank.

"Well, I know you think about him all the time. I hear you talking about him after I've gone to bed almost every night. You did last night, too, when you were drinking coffee in the kitchen."

"There is not much you miss, Elin, not so?" Äiti pinched her cheek and smiled. "And why do you lie awake to listen? You should be fast asleep."

"Äiti, do you know what I dreamed last night? I dreamed Grandfather and I were skating together in the arena. All the people were there and they clapped so hard."

Äiti held her close for a moment. "My girl want so to figure skate. My baby is fine, brave girl to give up money to Isä and Äiti."

"Now it's done, Äiti, I don't mind so much. And anyway, nobody else in Sudbury has a grandfather coming all the way from Finland!"

The day came at last. *Something's going to happen today,* Elin thought, as she opened her eyes. *Something good!* Then she remembered. *Grandfather's coming from Finland!* The very hour was racing closer and closer! Like the train Grandfather was coming on. "I don't have to go to school today, either," she said to herself as she pulled on her stockings.

"Elin! After breakfast you will go down to station and ask what time train come from Montreal with Grandfather!" Äiti called from the bottom of the stairs. Elin could hear the coal crackling in the old cook-stove.

She was soon on the way, jogging past the radio station. The big black letters on the window, CKSO, grinned down at her. Wouldn't it be wonderful if they let her go in and tell everybody over the radio that Grandfather was coming from Finland? Wouldn't everybody be surprised? She raced past Silverman's and down Durham Street. She must remember to tell Grandfather that the streets downtown running north and south were named after governors-general of Canada, and all those east and west after trees. He would want to know that. There were the railway tracks and a lone engine shunting up and down along them.

She was puffing like the engine as she came to the C.P.R. station buildings. *I'll never find the right place,* she thought. *There are so many buildings.* So many little carts, too, with Royal Mail painted in big red letters on their sides. Then she saw the big man. He was looking up at the sky, hands behind his back and a red cap on his head. "Hello," he said. "How are you today?"

"I'm fine, thank you," Elin smiled shyly. "Can you tell me where I find out about trains coming, please?"

"Ah sure can. You come this way with me." He reached down for her hand which Elin obediently tucked into his large black one, and they went around to the track side of the station. "Now you see this here board?" They stopped before a wide blackboard on the brick wall. "This here tells you. Now what train are you interested in?"

What a soft voice he has, Elin thought, peeking up at his dark face. She looked at the blackboard. So many names were scrawled on it in white chalk. "Sault Sainte Marie, Toronto, Vancouver," Elin read them aloud to the man. Did trains passing through Sudbury really go all the way to Vancouver? She'd seen Vancouver in the geography book and it was away on the other side of Canada! "Montreal, that's the one," she added.

"Montreal," the man was saying. "Let me see. Montreal six-forty A.M. That's tomorrow mornin', six-forty A.M. You goin' somewhere, child?"

"My Grandfather's coming all the way from Finland on that train," Elin announced with pride. "You know where Finland is?"

"Ah reckon it's far enough away for me to be mighty surprised, anyway. But you come along with me. If it's that important we'd better go and ask Mister Fulton." He guided her through the door to the waiting room, where two ladies were chatting and a man lounged in a shiny leather chair, a suitcase at his feet. Then the man called through the wicket, "Here's a young lady for you to look after, Mister Fulton. She's got mighty important news."

"Hello, what's all this, George?" Mr. Fulton had a green shade over his eyes. He peered out of his wicket at Elin. "Important news?"

"Her grandfather's comin' all the way from Finland, Mister Fulton, and he's comin' on the Montreal train. You tell her what time, will you?"

"Six-forty A.M., young lady," Mr. Fulton replied. "You coming to meet him?"

"I don't know. Maybe. If Äiti will let me."

"Well, I'll be here then, so come and say hello to me, won't you?" Mr. Fulton winked at George. "Too bad you're not going to be here, George, to help Grandfather off with his bags."

"It sure is, Mister Fulton. It sure is!"

Elin ran all the way home. She rushed into the kitchen and began to tell Äiti about Mister Fulton and the man called George. "What is it you're making, Äiti? It smells so good!"

"This is piirakka." Äiti rolled out her bread dough again and covered the meat in the deep dish with it. "Oh my, he will look good when he come out of oven. All golden brown and crusty. Grandfather will want much these dishes of Finland after two weeks on sea."

"Are we going to have kaali kääryleita, too, Aiti?"

"Yes, baby, I make the kaali kääryleita, the cabbage roll, tomorrow. Grandfather is like kaali kääryleita much, Elin."

"I don't think our kitchen ever smelled so good before," Elin sniffed happily.

That night Elin went to bed very early. She folded her clothes carefully over the back of the chair, where she could crawl into them quickly. She was going to the station with Isä to meet Grandfather. Äiti would stay at home with Juhani. She had heard Äiti say very quietly to Isä, "You will go with Elin, Lemmin. If I go I weep much. Better that I wait here and greet Isä with happiness. I shall keep hot the coffee."

Elin lay very still. The grey night peered in at her bedroom window. It was like going to bed on Christmas Eve. The little house was wrapped tight with suspense. *I won't go to sleep at all,* Elin decided. *If I do Isä might forget to wake me up at five o'clock and go to the station alone.* She counted the cars skimming down Finland Street by the gleam of light skipping in through the window, across the ceiling and out again. One! Maybe that was Mr. Polaszk and Peter, going home from the movies. They always went together in the middle of the week. Two! That must be Mrs. Venna's Ralph, coming home from the Legion Hall. Now when would the next one come? She must keep her eyes open. She *must.* There it was. But it wasn't at all like the others. It was a great ship sailing in through the window, all lighted up from stem to stern, and there was a man standing at the prow, waving and smiling. He had a pair of skates over his arm. Why, it was Grandfather! And he was calling to her! But the ship was moving away out through the window again. Someone was shaking it and the lights were trembling. Shaking! Shaking!

"Elin! Elin! It is time, little one!" Who was it? Where was she? She must try to speak. Grandfather was calling!

"Elin! Elin baby. Come now. It is time we go to meet Grandfather."

A dazzling light danced in her eyes. Why, it was only her own bedroom light. And there she was in her own little iron bed, with Isä patting her on the shoulder.

"Come, Elin, sleepy-head. I go down and have some coffee while you get dressed." The stairs creaked mysteriously as Isä slipped out into the darkness of the hall.

Elin stumbled to the floor, shivering. Her green dress did not want to be put on. It slipped and slithered this way and that as she pulled it over her head. She felt a little sick and wobbly. But there! Both her stockings were on and she was ready. She crept downstairs in the deep stillness.

When they stepped out into the darkness it was raining, and the wet wooden sidewalk shone in the circle of the street lamps. She felt the hard, familiar knobs of Isä's hand as they hurried along, their shoes scrunching strangely on the boards. She walked close to Isä. The dark and the silence were a little frightening and it was queer being up so early. Isä put his arm around her shoulders. "What is matter? My little girl tired, eh? Soon we be there. See, over there the station."

That huddle of lights was the railroad station and, as they drew nearer, she could hear the friendly sound of the engines shunting on the tracks, and the bells clanging close by. "Isä," she said softly. "There is no way Grandfather could get lost, is there? He's sure to be on this train, isn't he?"

"You ever hear of train getting lost, little one?" Isä chuckled.

"Well, no, I guess not, Isä. Trains are on tracks. How could they get lost anyway?"

"Sure, true that is," Isä agreed. "Well, baby, Grandfather is old by seventy-five years, lots older than the train. He know even better than trains how to look after himself. Don't worry. Here we are at station and when a few minutes pass, the train come."

They stepped through the door into the waiting-room. How long ago it seemed that she had passed through that very door with Mr. George. There were more people here now. One old lady was snoring a little, her head thrown back against the seat and her mouth wide open. Three men across the aisle chatted in low tones. One of them nodded in a friendly way at Isä as he and Elin sat down. "You folks taking the six-forty?" he smiled.

"No, we wait for visitor come, thank you," Isä answered. "Elin, perhaps you go and ask if train on time, please?"

Elin stepped up to the wicket. There was Mister Fulton, just as he had said he would be, writing very fast with a thick pencil. "Is the train for twenty to seven on time, please?" She peered through the wicket.

"Right on time. Right on time. You want a ticket?" Mr. Fulton shuffled through his papers without looking up.

A ticket? Had he forgotten about Grandfather coming from Finland? "I'm waiting for Grandfather," Elin announced in a clear, firm voice. "He's coming all the way from Finland. Don't you remember?"

"Well, my goodness gracious me!" Mr. Fulton dropped his papers and looked out. "So it's you. This is pretty early for a young lady like you to be up and about." He reached into the big lunch box beside him and produced a large, shiny red apple. "Here's a little something to chew on till that train gets in." He handed the apple to Elin. "You had your breakfast yet?"

Elin sidled to the wicket and took the gift, shyly. "Thank you very much. No, I haven't had my breakfast yet. It's too early. I'm waiting to eat mine with Grandfather." She clutched the apple tightly in her hand. *I'll have something to give Grandfather now*, she thought. She wondered if the station man would mind.

She was walking over to sit down with Isä again when someone called, "Here she comes!" Everyone rushed out to the platform.

Outside was a world of steam and clanging bells. Elin held one hand against her ear and grasped Isä's with the other. The train was shuddering slowly to a stop along the tracks. A strong smell of smoke and soot mingled with the drizzle. A broad-shouldered man passed them, pushing a heavy cart along right beside a freight car with Canadian Pacific Spans the World printed on it in big white letters. Huge sacks and bundles and boxes were thrown from the train to the cart. Elin watched in amazement. What wonderful things were in those boxes? Where had they all come from? *Maybe Grandfather's letters came in one of those big grey bags*, she thought. *This must happen every morning early, while I'm still fast asleep.*

"Isä, where will he get off?" But Isä didn't answer. He held her hand tightly and began to run. Elin could feel her coat flapping about her legs. There was a funny, tight knot in her throat that made it hard to breathe. Through the dim light she saw, away down at one end of the train, the conductor helping people to the ground. First came a lady with a baby in her arms, and as they hurried past Elin could hear the baby crying, just like Juhani. There! There was a man! But no. That couldn't be Grandfather. He wasn't old enough. Then a tall, straight figure in a brown coat was getting off the train. His hand groped for the railing. He felt his way carefully to the platform. Isä rushed up to him. They flung their arms about one another!

"Isä! Isä! Olet onnellisesti perilla!"

"Et ole muuttunut, olet sama, Lemmin, kun ennen. Mutta missä on Miina?"

"Kotona, Isä, han odottaa kotona!"

Grandfather did not even notice Elin. She pulled at the tabs on his pocket. "Grandfather," she called. "I'm here, too. See me? I'm Elin, Grandfather!"

Grandfather looked down. Elin blinked up at him sleepily. Then he lifted her in his arms, murmuring softly. "Miina's baby. This is Miina's baby."

Elin started to cry a little with the excitement but suddenly she remembered the apple and pushed it into Grandfather's hand. "That's a present for you," she whispered. "The station man gave it to me and I saved it for you."

Grandfather held her high in his arms, gave her a big kiss on both cheeks and put her down. Then he said in very careful and very halting English, "That is very wonderful gift for me. You are nice like I thought Miina's baby would be."

"Why, Isä!" Isä gazed at Grandfather in surprise. "You speak the English like us. Where you learn that?"

Grandfather drew himself up proudly, like a small boy who has been especially clever at his lessons. "For whole year I know I am come to see you here. So we get many book from town and I study very hard the English. How I do now? Almost as good as in the Finnic, do I not then?"

"Oh, Grandfather!" Elin clapped her hands with joy. "Oh, I'm so glad you've come!"

"My bags come later they tell me," Grandfather explained as they started off, hand in hand, up the street.

"Not much I bring but few bags."

I'm so tired, Elin thought suddenly, clinging tightly to Grandfather's hand as they plodded home through the light rain. The sidewalk was not wide enough for all three of them but they walked closely, Isä hopping up and down like a great toad, as they crowded him too far over on his side of the pavement.

It's like a dream, Elin fancied, as Grandfather and Isä fell silent. *Maybe I'll wake up and find I'm still in my bedroom with the cracks in the plaster, and I'll have to get ready for school.*

But it really was Grandfather speaking again. "Look! See!" he was saying softly. "Day is come here." He nodded towards the east where the rooftops looked like black cardboard cutouts against the cold grey dawn. Then he looked towards the west, where the rolling rock hills were solid black humps with a strange red light flaming behind them. "No!" Grandfather stopped suddenly. "There must be the sun, over there. Such redness I have not seen with a sun. It come so swift!"

Elin looked to where the sky was a wild red lake breaking in crimson waves from the west. She tugged at Grandfather's hand. She knew and he didn't! She could tell Grandfather something he didn't know on his very first day here! "That's the Giant Slag, Grandfather! That's not the sun!"

"It is only the slag they dump from the smelter over there, Grandfather." Isä smiled at him over Elin's head.

They stood quietly, watching. The light flared again and again across the sky, and faded slowly to a glimmer, like a huge live coal smouldering in the rock hills. "You will tell me all about it soon, Elin? This Giant Slag?" Grandfather began to walk on again, slowly. "That is beauty, I think. That is much beauty."

Then they were on Finland Street and the door was open, and Äiti was waiting there with tears running down her face. There was much talk and much laughter and many tears. Then Elin was suddenly very tired, and all she remembered was Grandfather laying her gently on her bed and whispering through her sleep, "Miina's baby. This is Miina's baby."

12

A Tale of the Trolls

"Oh, yes, Mrs. Venna. This is a great and wonderful country, and I am very happy to have come." Grandfather was sitting on the verandah with Juhani on his knee. He was bundled in an old blue coat of Isä's, and his black cap was pulled down well over his head to shut out the frosty fall air. Down the street danced the leaves of the birches, blown from the rock hills. Mrs. Venna was raking the leaves into a great heap. She would carry them in a wheelbarrow around the back to her little garden.

"And our Finland, Grandfather," Mrs. Venna spoke to Grandfather in Finnish, "is she still as beautiful as ever?"

Grandfather's eyes shone, and his face, clean scrubbed, shone as brightly as his blue eyes. "Finland, Mrs. Venna, Finland will always be for me the most beautiful country in the world."

"It is a little like Finland, this Canada, Grandfather," Mrs. Venna nodded. "These lakes — these birch trees. But it is not the same."

Grandfather shook his head wisely. "Nothing is the same as the homeland, Mrs. Venna. Nothing! But for Elin and for this baby," he beamed down at Juhani playing on his knee, and at Elin, hunched up on the top step, "for these babies, this Canada is the homeland, and for them it, too, will be beautiful."

"Up! Up!" Juhani held his two chubby arms toward Elin. She sprang up and cradled him like a huge doll. "Grandfather's talking about us," she whispered through his woollen cap. "You better be good, and maybe one day Grandfather will tell us a story all about Finland." She jigged him up and down breathlessly.

"Hyvää paivää, Grandfather!" Mrs. Venna lumbered off heavily with her last wheelbarrow full of yellow birch leaves.

"Hyvää paivää, Mrs. Venna."

"That means good day, Juhani. Say 'good day' to Mrs. Venna." Elin lifted his mittened hand and waved it. Juhani gurgled with laughter and waved by himself. *She looks like the brown bear Isä and I saw eating berries in the bush last summer,* Elin thought, *all bundled in her thick brown coat, with the brown kerchief tied over her hair.*

But Grandfather was not always content to sit on the front verandah and watch the people passing by. One day after school he took Elin's hand and said, "Come, little one. Do you wish to take Grandfather for small walk to see your city? I see big rocks I like to climb. Maybe you take me there, too, please?"

Together they set out down Finland Street. They came to Mr. Kurtsheff's store, and the fat grocer was sitting out on the front stoop. Over his apron he wore an old red sweater fastened with one last button. Elin took Grandfather up the steps. "This is my Grandfather, and he's come all the way from Finland, Mr. Kurtsheff."

Mr. Kurtsheff set his chair back on its four legs and

struggled to his feet. "That's Grandfather, what's coming all the way from Finland? Mine goodness! Pleased to meeting you, I'm sure." He held out his hand and Grandfather shook it warmly. "You're liking our country here, Grandfather?" Mr. Kurtsheff sat down again and pulled his sweater more closely around him.

"It is great country, I think," replied Grandfather, very slowly to be sure of his English words. "Elin is now show me your city and the rocks maybe."

"Ah, there is no place like the old lands, Grandfather. Mine Vienna, what would I give to seeing it again once more!"

"You come from Austria then, my friend?"

"Mine father is best butcher in all Vienna." Mr. Kurtsheff was happy to tell his tale to someone new. "Ever been to Vienna, Grandfather?"

"I come nowhere but here. Finland is very beautiful land and there is no reason to leave. Only to see my daughter and the babies I come."

"And how is the skating lessons mit mine Elin? You being the champeen figure skater of the world yet, Elin?"

"How's business these days, Mr. Kurtsheff?" said Elin, changing the subject rapidly.

"Business is okay, I'm thanking you, Elin." Mr. Kurtsheff winked at Grandfather. "Of course we don't sell as much ice cream cones and candies as once, when we have little Elin to looking after the ice cream counter. But on the whole, business is okay."

Grandfather chuckled and turned to Elin. "We shall go now please, Elin?" He shook Mr. Kurtsheff's hand warmly again. "You have much happiness here, friend. You have great new country to look after, and you have babies like this to look after, too." He motioned to Elin standing silently beside him. "She is this new land, and it is for her and the little ones who are her friends. Be of kindness to them, Mr. Kurtsheff."

"That's very nice, very nice, I'm sure." Mr. Kurtsheff leaned back in his wooden chair against the store front, as Grandfather and Elin went off down the street. "Grandfather is such nice man!"

"Now what is this about skating lesson? And the champion figure skater, Elin?" Grandfather tried to look down into Elin's face.

"We'll have to hurry if we're going to climb the Pinnacle before dark, Grandfather." Elin pretended to be very interested in the things in the window of the drug store they were passing.

"And where is this Pinnacle, please?" Grandfather nodded wisely to himself.

"Just around the corner and two streets over."

"What is this fine, new place, Elin?" Grandfather looked with interest at a large grey stone building. He stopped to read a bronze tablet next to the doorway. "Inco. What is this 'Inco'?"

"Inco is just about the most important thing around here, I guess." Elin peered through the glass door. "Inco means International Nickel Company and they own the mines. This big building is the club for the men who work for the company. They have parties here, and plays and dances, too."

Grandfather and Elin turned on to Elm Street, passed the *Sudbury Daily Star* Building and the Nickel Range Hotel.

"Hi, Elin!"

Elin held her breath while Anna dashed across the street between the cars and bicycles.

"I've just been shopping for Mom. Say! I bet this is Grandfather from Finland!"

"You are smart girl," Grandfather approved. "And this could be perhaps Anna, of whom I hear so much?"

"You're smart, too, Grandfather." Elin eyed him with pride. "How did you know this was Anna?"

"How could I not know Anna, with the pretty red hair all curls, when I hear so much about it?" Grandfather stooped to shake hands gravely.

"Well, I'm glad you got here. I never saw a famous man before." Anna stared at Grandfather with great interest and shifted her parcel of groceries to the other arm. "I have to go in to Kresge's before it closes, so I better go. G'bye now!"

"Goodbye, Anna!" They passed the two corners to Cedar Street and walked quickly by Loblaws' huge window and several apartment houses. Elin stopped and pointed to the end of the avenue. "There it is, Grandfather! There's the Pinnacle! It looks just like the end of an ice cream cone, only it's dark grey."

Grandfather's eyes looked where Elin's finger pointed. High up, rising above the birches, was a great mound of rock, tapering to a slim peak.

"That is good climb for Grandfather. It will take the breath."

In a few moments they reached the end of the sidewalk and the rock loomed up before them like a vast wall of grey slate.

"It's awfully stony up here, Grandfather!" They picked their way carefully through the dwarfed birch trees, silent and still, like yellow mist in the setting sun.

"Ooooh! Help!" Elin's foot slipped and she began to slide backward.

Grandfather was behind her and gave her a big push. She made her way to the next rock in safety. "It's only a little way now," she puffed.

At the top they sat down with a deep sigh and rested silently until they found their breath again. Here, they were curled up on a ledge of rock where the silver birches and the scarlet sumachs gathered in gay clusters to make a glen. Through a large opening in the branches they could see Sudbury City, a haze of smoke and roof tops far below.

"This is the place for the trolls, is it not, little one?" Grandfather observed.

"I don't know what you mean."

"You never hear of the trolls?" Grandfather was so astonished that Elin was ashamed. Why hadn't she studied harder at school? Then she might have known. "You never hear of the fairies, too? You have not the fairies in Canada, Elin?"

"Oh, goodness, yes. But I know there aren't really fairies in Canada. They're just in story-books."

Grandfather looked a little hurt. "So, Miina's baby does not believe in the fairies. Well, I can say, little one, there are fairies in Suomi, in our good Finland. And Grandfather has seen them with his own eyes, too."

"You really and truly have seen a *fairy*, Grandfather? A real live *fairy*, like what we read about in books?"

"With my two eyes I see the fairies. Only it was not the fairy like we call fairy. It was trolls. How you say here? Like the little man, all dress in brown and green with long big cap on his head."

"That's a goblin, Grandfather!"

"Goblin, that is it," Grandfather agreed. "Only not one but many goblins. It all happen very long ago, when

Grandfather was small boy."

"Small like me maybe?" Elin's cornflower blue eyes shone with delight. "Were you just nine years old, too, Grandfather?"

"Oh, much more small than you, little one. It was my first year I go to school and I have big forest to go through to get there." A smile crinkled the corners of the kind eyes that were gazing through the trees, far down the years, over the sea to Finland.

"It was winter evening," Grandfather continued. "In Suomi the nights come swift, and the snow fall thick and slow, filling the air with great silence. I come home through the forest from my school following the path made by the pulkka in the snow. Pulkka is low, wooden sled we use in Finland," he explained, seeing a question in Elin's eyes. "I run, for I have work to do for my Isä before the meal, and I am late from school this day. But sudden I stop. A song come across the snow, a very sweet song that come and go, faint, through the falling snow. I stand very still for a little and wait. There is no more song. Then I start to run on, and sudden, there it is again, like a bell, ringing soft, far, far away. So I follow this music, and as I follow it, it get more and more loud, like many small people sing at festival time. There is very small glen, like this one where we sit, of pine and birch. I see tiny lights flash among the trees and I creep up on the hand and the knee to look. They are there, all dance and sing together round a ring of fire."

"Who was there, Grandfather?" Elin leaned so close to him that she almost pushed him off the ledge in her excitement.

"Why, the trolls, of course! There is one in the middle more big than the others, and he beat out time on a big,

big stone that sound hollow. All the others dance and sing around him. I was so little boy I think I call them and see if they will let me go to them. But just as I begin to get up to my feet, a great thing come! There is a big, big noise, like I have never heard, and like I hear not again. A big crash bang and there, standing beside the rock is big, big man! How you say that, Elin?"

"A giant, Grandfather?"

"A giant stand there with great hammer in hand and hit the rock till all the fire fly from it. He give three great strikes with hammer and all the air is fire and snow all mixed and big sound. Then it all go. Quick! Just like you snap your finger."

Elin shivered.

"All go. And the snow is fall, silent and slow again, and there is only big rock in middle of little glen and silly Grandfather on his knee looking through trees."

"Did you tell your Äiti and Isä about it, Grandfather?"

"At first I do not tell them. I think they laugh at me for being little boy. They think I tell story only. But then I tell them just before I go to bed."

"And what did your Isä say? Had he ever seen the trolls in the forest?"

"He say, 'That is Ilmarinen, the mighty smith of the forest, and his helpers you see. I see them once, too, when I am little boy like you.'"

"Did you ever see them again, Grandfather? The trolls and the giant?"

"Never again. Sometime I think I hear the music again, but when I try to find it, it go far, far away, and I find only snow and trees and darkness."

"I don't think anybody's seen any fairies or goblins

here." Elin looked away over the valley. The lights of Sudbury were winking on, one by one. Suddenly she grasped Grandfather's arm and pointed to the west. "Look, Grandfather! See? Over there on the hill. It's the Giant Slag again!"

"So! You have the giants here in Canada and not the trolls, little one?"

"He's just a make-believe giant, Grandfather," Elin laughed. "When I look at the rocks I can see a great big giant lying on his side sleeping, and when the slag comes, it's just as if he's dipping his brush in a pot of fire and painting the sky. See?"

The birch trees stood like tall black candles and the last few golden leaves tapered to a pale flame. But beyond them a greater flame was glowing. The giant of the rock hills was busy once again with his painting. Stream after stream of his fire poured down the hillside.

"It look to me as if the giant upset his paint-pot," Grandfather smiled. "There is so much of this brightness."

Quietly they watched while it glowed like a mighty forge in the darkness, then slowly faded to a faint glimmer and was gone.

"It is like the smithy of Ilmarinen, himself," Grandfather murmured. "And how you say this slag come, Elin?"

"Well, it's what's left over after they've melted all the nickel out of the rock. That's what the teacher told us. And it's no good any more, so they just dump it in little trucks and throw it down the hill while it's still hot."

"For a thing that is no good, it makes much beauty," Grandfather said softly. "It is like the night of the midnight sun, when it comes over the hill."

"What's the night of the midnight sun, please, Grandfather? I know about the midnight sun. That's where the sun never goes to bed all night. It's away up in the north country where it's very cold. But what's the night of the midnight sun?"

Grandfather scrambled to his feet. "It is late, little one. You get cold sitting up here, for soon the frost come. School tomorrow and Elin must be wide awake and thinking clear. Come! Some other day we hear of this night of the midnight sun, eh?"

Grandfather went first, feeling his way down across the ridges and helping Elin down after him. The trees closed about them in quietness as they stepped down. The clip-clop of their feet made a friendly sound on the cement sidewalk. The warm, familiar smell of soot and smoke drifted with them along Cedar Street. They walked home, hand in hand, through the early twilight, watching the first faint twinkle of the stars.

13

The Giant Slag's Secret

"Hey, Elin! Wait for me!" Grandfather, Stepan and Elin whirled around, startled.

"It's only Anna." Stepan pushed his hair out of his eyes and began to saunter on again.

"Well, let's wait," Elin suggested, "if it's Anna."

"I saw you coming round Finland Street corner," Anna panted. "But you didn't hear me yell. Where are you going anyway? It'll soon be dark."

"Grandfather wanted to see what Frood Mine looked like, so Stepan and I are taking him out."

"Can I come, too?" Anna was still puffing. "I was supposed to go to the movies with Chrissie but she can't go. So I'll just go out to Frood with you."

"Gosh, another girl!" Stepan muttered.

"We must hurry then." Grandfather started up the road again with the three of them crowding close around him. "It is no good trying to see things when the dark is come."

"Huh," Anna grunted. "Tell that to Stepan. He's the old poke."

They walked briskly along the winding road and up the hill, past the rock-strewn valley. "And what is all this?" Grandfather pointed to the rocks piled gaunt and high beside the road like the ruins of the old castle in the history book.

"That's what they call 'fill'." Stepan was proud of his knowledge. "It's what's left over after they've blasted out the rock the nickel is in, and the copper, too. See over there? That's where the open pit is."

"Open pit?" Grandfather was entirely confused. "What is open pit, please?"

"Well, Grandfather," Elin grasped his hand firmly as they strode along the road together, "in the mine there's men like Isä finding nickel underneath the ground, 'way down underneath, and there's men finding nickel on top of the earth. On top is the open pit. But you can't see it from here."

"Look now!" shouted Stepan. "There's the truck bringing up some more fill."

Over to the west a huge truck, its sides bulging with rock, was toiling up the steep incline like an enormous ant struggling along with its load to the ant hill.

"They'll dump it now," Anna advised. "You just wait. The back of the truck will come down. See? There it goes!" They stood silently watching, as in the distance the barren rock poured from the truck, to make the heap on the hill even larger.

"Away down in the hole where we can't see," Elin went on, "they blast about twice a day with dynamite — big blasts to get the rock out that has the nickel in it."

"Ah, so that is the big noise I hear then," Grandfather nodded. "At first I am a little scared."

"That's what makes the cracks in my bedroom wall, too," Elin said.

"Pop says the blasts sometimes crack windows in the building at Frood," Anna put in.

"They are big blasts then," Grandfather agreed. "What happen to all this rock with the nickel in it what these men blast?"

"First of all it's crushed small in rock crushers," Stepan explained. "See those smoke stacks over there on the top of the rocks? That's the smelter at Copper Cliff. All the rock's taken over there and melted in the big furnaces. Then the copper and nickel and gold and all the other metals come out."

"Ah, I know now. I remember Elin told me. This slag we see at night. This sight of much beauty in the sky. That is the rock left over when the nickel is taken out. They throw it away while it is still hot and burning." Grandfather was triumphant at having discovered the complete secret of the slag. He gazed silently at the smoke stacks which seemed to be climbing the far hill. "They are big, these stacks. Is like a big ship sail across the sky, with smoke flying."

"That's just what I thought, too, Grandfather," Elin smiled up at him. "Just like the ship you came on from Finland."

"They're so big at the top that a car can ride around on them," Stepan hastened to say. "And the teacher says they're the biggest in the British Empire. One of them is five hundred and ten feet high."

"I guess Copper Cliff is pretty important all right." Anna jerked at the end of Stepan's shirt-tail, dangling below his jacket. "I guess it's just as important as Sudbury, even if it is smaller, because that's where the nickel gets ready to be sent off around the world."

"Look there!" They had come suddenly to the top of

the hill and Grandfather stopped in amazement. "A little town all alone!"

"That's Frood, Grandfather," Anna laughed. "That's where all the men who are head of the mine live. And see that red brick building?" She pointed toward a long, flat building, running along the opposite side of the road.

"What is that, please?"

"That's the mine building," Elin explained. "In there are all the engine shops, carpenter's shops and everything. That's what Isä told me."

They drew close to the building. Streams of water sprang from a great concrete floor and fell again with a gentle swish to the ground. Grandfather looked expectantly at Stepan.

"I think the water has something to do with working the engines inside, Grandfather. But see, over there, that big, tall building going down into the earth? I know for sure what that is. That's where the air is pumped down into the mine all the time, so the miners won't suffocate. It's fun to watch the water, though."

They stood listening to the sound of the water gushing forth and retreating. Then Grandfather wandered along to the back of the iron fence. "What is that tall building there, beyond the flat one?"

"That's the shaft house, where Isä and all the men who work in the mine get into cages and go down every day. They're down there now, 'way, 'way down, perhaps half a mile." Elin shivered. "I wouldn't want to be a miner. Not a bit."

"Well, I would." Stepan eyed her with scorn. "I'd love to go 'way down there. It'd be real fun riding down in that funny elevator and blasting the rock. You know what I'd like to do? My father told me you can walk ten miles under the ground in the mines. I'd like to do that. Soon as I'm through school I'm going to be a miner," he boasted. "I'm going to use a big drill like my Dad did."

"Well, I guess you won't have to know much then," Anna snorted. "You're kind of dumb at school."

"It is well some one wish to go down these mines, Anna," Grandfather reproved. "Or how we get the nickel? Some people is good at one thing, some at another. They are brave men, these miners."

Stepan's brave, too, Elin thought. *He isn't afraid of snakes and things. And he's lots of fun, even if he isn't so good at school.*

"Yes, and nickel is important, too," Stepan was telling them. "Teacher says they mix it with other metals to make them stronger. She told us once about a plough made of nickel, used under the ocean."

"A plough use under the water?" Grandfather raised his fair bushy eyebrows.

"It's used to dig a deep hole all across the ocean floor, so the cables that carry the telegraph messages can be laid there. Then ships don't bump into the cables and break them."

"That is wonderful. Wonderful!" Grandfather looked pleased with Stepan. Suddenly there was a distant roar above their heads. Far above them, winging across the blue-green sky, an airplane soared towards the stars. "There is another place nickel go," Grandfather cried. "Up in air! Nickel help make airplane, too!"

"And trains, and buses, and trucks and stoves and pipes and . . . " Anna paused for breath.

"And pot cleaners!" Stepan announced triumphantly. "That's what it says on Mom's box of pot cleaners at home."

"Isä told me that even in the mines, nickel mixed with other stuff makes the cages and elevators in the mines stronger, the elevators that lift up the ore, I mean," Elin declared. "I guess nickel *is* important."

"I think you live in very important place, little ones," Grandfather reminded them. "People tell me there is more nickel here in Sudbury than anywhere else in the wide world."

"Say, did you know nine-tenths of the world's nickel comes from Sudbury?" Stepan poked Anna in the back.

"You sound like an old schoolbook!" Anna teased.

"Well," Stepan defended himself, "maybe I'm not so dumb either."

"It seem to me that Stepan is very smart with the figures." Grandfather nodded at Stepan in admiration.

Stepan grinned down at his boots. "Aw, I don't know."

"Wait now!" Grandfather called. "Before we go, what is all this wood, on the ground behind big building?"

"Isä says they use it to build the big beams across the tunnels in the mine, so the rock doesn't fall in on them," Elin said. "They build the railways under the ground with it, too."

"It is great city, this Sudbury. This Canada have many fine thing!" Stepan grinned at Elin and Anna as Grandfather chatted to himself.

Clip-clop! Clip-clop! sounded their boots again on the road to the city. Suddenly Stepan grabbed Grandfather's arm and pointed toward the west. "There's the slag, Grandfather! They're dumping the slag!"

"Our Giant Slag." Grandfather looked at Elin. She nodded and smiled. "Is it not strange, little ones," he went on, "to think we stand now over rock that may tomorrow be poured down the hill over there as slag?"

"Once Pop took me right out to where they dump the slag," Anna boasted. "It was all sort of scary."

"Aw, girls you're scared of everything!" Stepan snickered.

"What happened, Anna? What does it look like up close?" Elin tugged anxiously at Anna's plump arm.

"I, too, would like to know, Anna," Grandfather encouraged her, smiling. "What you see there?"

"Well, there's a little train with a lot of big pots fastened one behind the other. It runs along a track to the place on the rocks where the slag is being dumped." Anna remembered all about it. "Then, when it gets there, the man in the engine up front pulls a lever, and the first pot turns on its side and dumps the slag. It all pours down the black hill, flaming like fire. Then the next pot is dumped, and the next and the next, till they're all empty. And do you know what it looks like when it's dark?" Anna drew a deep, dramatic breath.

"No, what?" Stepan was interested, in spite of himself.

"Just like the bones of a dozen skeletons all on fire, lying on the black rocks." Anna shivered. "It's scary at first but I guess I wouldn't be scared if I went out to see it again."

Grandfather patted her shoulder gently.

"You know, Grandfather, it's so hot that even standing out on the roadway you can feel warm all over from the heat of the slag," Anna told him. "And when all the other fire went out, one little piece of slag burned all by itself like a big, shiny eye."

Grandfather was watching the last light shimmering over the sleeping giant. "So is more nickel made ready for the world," he said quietly. Then he took Anna's and Elin's hands firmly in his own, and they walked, swift and sure, down the road to the city. Stepan plodded along behind, kicking at Anna's heels.

14

Christmas in Finland

The long, mellow autumn days came to an end one Saturday in November. "It will be an early and a hard winter!" The old people pulled their coats more closely about them, as the cold wind swept down across the rocklands to Sudbury and Finland Street.

"The trees will be cold, too." Grandfather looked at the fragments of leaves clinging to the silver birches on the hillside. Elin sat with him at the kitchen window after the breakfast dishes were washed and put away.

Suddenly she pressed her nose against the cold windowpane. "Grandfather! It's snowing! It's the first snow!"

"That will fill in all holes in rock and cover poor bare trees." Grandfather leaned closer to see the big, lacy flakes drifting silently down. "Tell Grandfather, little one. Yesterday morning I go down to lake and I see funny veil hang all over lake water. They look like ghost waving and I stand and watch. What is that, please?"

"Those aren't ghosts, Grandfather," Elin laughed. "Teacher says it's called Arctic Smoke. It comes all the time in the fall because the water is warmer than the air. That's what it is. Like clouds on the water."

"Ah, so I learn new thing. That is good, little one."

Now every morning was still and crisp, with the smoke rising in straight, silent columns from the chimneys. The nights were suddenly alive with the strange echo of frost cracking in all the little clapboard houses on Finland Street, like the guns of an army of unseen little people.

"And what is this pop so sudden?" Grandfather looked up with a start from reading his paper by the stove, the first time he heard the sound.

"Pop?" Elin looked puzzled. "What do you mean 'pop'?"

"The big pop I hear just now."

"It is the frost, Grandfather." Isä glanced up from washing his hands at the kitchen sink. "The frost make the noise in the house, cracking the nails and the walls. You see it on the roofs in the mornings."

"Yes, I see him on the roof, this Mr. Frost. It look as if the whole house is full of smoke, and it creep out all over the top. This Mr. Frost play funny trick on me. I know him the next time."

Not long after, Elin came running home from school one day, and found Grandfather clearing the snow from the front walk. "Hello! Hello!" he called.

"Grandfather, do you know what?" Elin plunged through a snowdrift and flung her schoolbag on the verandah steps. "We're having a Christmas party at school in our room, just before the Christmas holidays. Today we drew for names and I got Willie Dixon's."

"And what this draw the name for?" Grandfather heaved another mound of snow from the walk. "What happen to Willie Dixon?"

"I have to buy him a present for the Christmas tree.

We all draw names from a box at school, and the name we get we buy the present for."

"And do this cost much money, Elin?"

"Twenty-five cents! Stepan got Chrissie's name and he's mad, 'cause he says he's not going to buy any old girl a Christmas present. But Wendy said he'd just better buy one!"

"I think it is fine idea." Grandfather rested on his shovel to get his breath. "And what you buy with this twenty-five cents?"

"Oh, almost anything. Elizabeth says she hopes she gets candy, but I'm like Yolande, I don't really care what I get. I'll like it anyway. Oh, I love Christmas, Grandfather!"

"Yes, Christmas is come and Grandfather almost forget." He began to shovel snow again. "One day we must go down and see lake before Christmas come, eh? And the place where the skating is?"

The next Saturday was a crisp, clear day. The sun made a thousand diamonds on the snow slopes. In the afternoon Grandfather and Elin put on their snow-boots and much warm clothing. "It is time now we go to see the lake in the winter." Grandfather grasped Elin's hand and they set off down the road in the snow.

"I like it when the sidewalk gets all covered up and we have to walk in the road." Elin gazed around her at the snow piled high on the sidewalks. "And the nice crunchy sound our boots make in the snow."

They stepped along the path used by the skaters. It brought them, very soon, to the edge of the lake, where the boys had cleared a great clean patch of ice. At one end they were playing hockey and at the other, a group of children were spinning along, some of them arm in arm, on the smooth ice surface.

"Look, Elin! The boys skate here." Grandfather's face broke into a broad, happy smile. "And there are the girls, too. You have the skates, little one?"

"Mine are too small for me, Grandfather." Elin watched the skaters wistfully. "Maybe one day I'll get some more. You used to be a famous skater, didn't you, Grandfather? Äiti told me you were really famous and won all the prizes. Can you still do it now?"

"Not for many year I skate, Elin, but oh, I like to do it so much! But the skating is for the young person, like my Elin, when the body is strong, and can move with beauty over the ice. Now I must stand on side and give the clap to the boy and girl who do it like me."

"Anna can figure skate." Elin drew Grandfather into the shelter of the pines, out of the keen wind. "She's wonderful. I saw her skate once. And there were some more girls, too. Oh, Grandfather, it was lovely!" She was once again sitting on the bench at the arena, watching the four girls wing toward her on their magic skates. "It costs an awful lot of money to learn to skate, though," she added slowly. "I almost learned to skate once, too."

"You learn almost?" Grandfather pretended to be puzzled. "What you mean please, this learn almost?"

Elin shook her head. That was a secret, a deep secret between Isä and Äiti and Elin. "I wouldn't be very good at it, anyway."

"Never let me hear a child of Finland tell she is not good on skates, little one," Grandfather commanded sternly. Then he smiled again. "If you have the Finnish blood in the vein, you have the skating blood, too. Yes?"

"Yes, Grandfather," Elin agreed. "Then maybe some

day, when I get rich, I'll be a figure skater like you were. Anyway, I can skate all right on ordinary skates, if I had a pair to fit."

When they were plodding home slowly, one behind the other because the track was narrow, Elin's thoughts turned to Christmas. "Grandfather, what would you like to find best of all in your Christmas stocking?"

"How you mean, in my stocking, Elin?"

"Why, don't you hang up your stocking over there in Finland?"

"And why should I hang up the stocking, please?"

"So that Santa Claus can fill it, of course! Oh, Grandfather! You're so funny!"

"I do not hear before of this hanging the stocking, Elin. We have different way in Finland."

"Tell me about it, Grandfather, please. What do they do there?"

"Is Isä and Äiti not tell you what happen in Finland at Christmas, Elin?" Grandfather was surprised.

"I guess Isä and Äiti are too busy to tell me about Finland. And now they live in Canada we have Christmas the way everybody does in Canada."

They came to a wide smooth path of snow again and Grandfather took her little red-mittened hand in his and was silent for a moment, carefully choosing his English words. "It is like this, little one, the Christmas in the old land. Before, for all the week, the women scrub and clean till all shine. Then they mix all kinds good-smelling things and bake, till the mouth waters at all the fine smells in the house. Christmas evening come, and that is the holy night as well as the happy one. We go out and bring home the tree, and put it in front of the window. We draw back the curtain so all friends can see our tree. Over there, when I was little boy, we have not the lights like you have now, but we put candles on branches, and the good sweets and even tiny cakes, bake special for the tree. The candles are light and when it is dark, oh, the tree have so much beauty with the candlelight creeping out the window to the snow. And everybody go round from house to house, to see whose tree is most lovely, and all the lights shine out of the window." Elin plodded on silently beside Grandfather, her thoughts in far-away Suomi on the night before Christmas.

"That is very good night for the little ones. That is the night they do not go to bed at all. Santa Claus . . . that is what you say here, is it not?" Elin nodded. "Santa Claus come, one from every family."

"You mean there's more than one Santa Claus, Grandfather?"

"Yes, every family make one of its people into a Santa Claus and send him round to take the gift to all the other family. And this go on all the night long till morning come. And then there is much lovely sound of bells in the air, over the fields and through the forest. All the good people of Suomi are going to kirkko. That is the church, you know. They come from every place in their sleighs, with the sleighbells ring, and the church bells ring. And still do the candles shine over the snow, for it is very early in the morning, only six o'clock."

"That is a wonderful Christmas, Grandfather," Elin sighed. "I wish we had it like that here."

"And now you know Christmas in Suomi, little one, what are you want to find in your stocking, please?"

"Äiti says I may get a new pair of shoes for very best, if I'm good, that is. And if I'm specially good, maybe a new sweater coat, too."

Elin smiled up at Grandfather and they walked home happily together.

15

Anna Acts Strangely

"Grandfather, if you had to get a present for a boy in your class for twenty-five cents, what would you buy?" Elin drew a little Christmas tree on the corner of her notebook. She was leaning over the kitchen table doing her homework. Grandfather was reading the Finnish newspaper, his stocking feet propped up on the warm fender of the stove.

"It is trouble for me to say, Elin." Grandfather dropped the paper to his knee so he could think very hard. "Here I know not what twenty-five cents buy. Now, if only we go together to the store, perhaps I help you then."

"Oh, Grandfather, would you? Could we go tonight?" Elin hopped up so quickly that her chair toppled over.

Grandfather put his fingers to his lips and picked it up for her. "Let us try to be quiet, Elin, or we wake Isä. That would not do when he go to work at the midnight hour." He pulled her against his knee and lifted her chin with his gnarled hand. "Now tell me, how we shop tonight when the store is all close?"

"Oh, no, Grandfather! The stores aren't closed. They stay open till nine o'clock for two weeks before Christmas. Please let's go now, while Äiti's putting

Juhani to sleep. Please, Grandfather!" Elin felt so grown-up at the thought of going shopping after dark.

"Come then." Grandfather rose slowly to his feet. "If it is that much you wish to go, we go. On with the cap and the coat, Elin."

When they stepped out into the winter night they drew their coats more closely about them, for a bitter wind whistled over the rock hills and down Finland Street. But the street lamps gleamed a warm welcome and the light shimmered on the drifts of snow, piled like huge scoops of the white icing Äiti had prepared for the Christmas cakes.

"Now where we buy our gift?" Grandfather threaded his way through the crowds on Elm Street. "Where we spend this twenty-five cents?"

"Well, I guess Woolworth's or Kresge's would be best, Grandfather." Elin dodged a plump lady with an arm full of parcels. "They have the most for twenty-five cents. Oh, Grandfather, look!" She pulled him to a shop window. In the centre of a great roof top built right across the window rose a red chimney, and sitting right on top of the chimney was Santa Claus grinning out at them, with a huge pack of toys on his back. Elin and Grandfather stood entranced.

"Look, Grandfather! There's a box of paints sticking out of Santa's sack. I think a box of paints would be a good thing to get Willie Dixon, don't you? If I can get some for twenty-five cents."

"It is good thing, a box of paints." Grandfather motioned her away from the window to make room for three more children, trying to peer over their shoulders. "Come then to the store, and we see."

The warm air from Kresge's store covered them like

a shawl as they pushed in through the swinging door. The aisles were thronged with shoppers and they had to jostle their way through, Elin clinging tightly to Grandfather's hand so she would not lose him.

"Here's the toy counter, Grandfather!"

Dolls and carts, toy trains and gaily coloured books, jigsaw puzzles and penny banks, winding toys and tops lay before them in splendid confusion. "It looks just as if Santa Claus stopped here and dumped out his pack."

"It does, Elin," Grandfather agreed. "And see? A box of paints for twenty cents there. Is that not the thing now?"

They waited their turn for the girl to take their money and wrap the box of paints. Then they moved down the aisle to the door. They were pressing through the crowds at the jewellery counter when Elin tugged at Grandfather to stop. "Grandfather, there's Anna! She must be buying Christmas presents, too. Let's go and say hello to her." She elbowed a passage to the counter. "Hello, Anna. Grandfather and I are shopping, too. What are you buying?"

"I'm . . . uh . . . I'm . . . " Anna tucked her hand quickly behind her back. "Well . . . I'm just buying some things for the . . . uh . . . Christmas tree. What are you buying?"

"Grandfather and I just bought Willie Dixon a paint box for the Christmas tree at school." How strangely Anna was acting, almost as if she wished Elin hadn't come along at all. And she was blushing. "You going home soon?"

"Oh, no. Not for a long time. Don't wait for me. I'll be late, awful late."

"Come, Elin, we go and do perhaps more shopping, too." Grandfather took Elin's hand and steered her towards the door. He smiled over his shoulder at Anna. "Goodbye, Anna! We see you again!"

"Grandfather, something's the matter with Anna. She just acts as if she didn't want me for a friend any more." Elin's face clouded with disappointment. "I never did anything to her."

"We shall not worry over this, Elin." Grandfather pulled on his brown mittens again in the cold air at the doorway. "But you know I think it would be nice thing if we buy for Anna the Christmas present from Elin. Not so?"

"Oh, Grandfather! I'd love to buy Anna a Christmas present, but I haven't any money."

"Grandfather have the money, so we buy one. And this night, too. Now where we go for this present?"

"I think we should go over to Woolworth's, Grandfather," Elin moved to one side to let a man go in the store. "Come on, this way."

They crossed over to Durham Street and Elin took a running slide on an icy place outside the post office. She laughed to see Grandfather doing the same. "That is make me think of when I am small boy in Finland," he chuckled. "But look now. Here is Woolworth's."

Once again they wandered among the crowds, this time aimlessly for they did not know exactly what they wanted. The candy counter was heaped with rainbow-coloured candy and above it, on a string, hung big, thick Christmas stockings, bulging with candy kisses and toys. They were walking past the ribbon counter when Grandfather pulled Elin aside. "There, I see a thing maybe Anna like." He motioned to a tray full of brilliant hair bows, spread before them like the flashing wings of a dozen butterflies. "How pretty a green bow on Anna's red hair!"

"Grandfather, I just can't think of anything nicer than a big green bow for Anna's hair." Elin fingered the silk ribbons carefully. "But they cost twenty-five cents."

"We have the money enough." Grandfather's hand groped in his pocket and came out with a quarter.

"Let me carry the packages, Grandfather." With the Christmas treasures clutched closely in her mitten, Elin trudged home with Grandfather through the snow.

Christmas Eve came and more snow. The little house on Finland Street was bubbling with excitement. After supper Grandfather lifted his heavy jacket and cap from the hook. "Now if someone show me where is the axe, I go out and chop down the tree for Christmas."

"Oh, Grandfather!" Elin eyed him with surprise. "You don't go and chop trees down in Sudbury for Christmas. You have to go and buy them on the street corner."

"You are not in the good Finland now, Grandfather." Isä's laughter rang out from the kitchen corner where he was cleaning his shoes. "Around Sudbury there is not the tree for Christmas that is tall and big enough."

Grandfather removed his cap and sat down. "Then where is this tree come from that I buy on the street corner, please?"

Äiti rolled out some more cookie dough on the table. "Isä, it is not the same as at home where we all go out on night before Christmas, and choose the tree that is finest on our own land. Here the trees are chop down many months before, in the country north of here, and bring to the city for to sell."

Grandfather nodded his head. "Then we go to buy the Christmas tree, eh, Elin?"

Elin was soon bundled in her coat, with a blue scarf wound around her head. The whirling snow made great white stars on her collar, like the star in the Christmas story. They were coming around the corner near the Nickel Range Hotel when they heard music, drifting across the street like the echo of some far chimes. "Let's stop for a minute, Grandfather." Elin pulled him to the edge of the sidewalk so that they could see better.

On the opposite side of the street, in one of the store windows, hung a great white bell. It swung slowly back and forth, as if moved by an unseen hand, and chimed softly the notes of a Christmas carol. As the bell made the melody, a group of boys and girls outside the window sang the words.

Oh, little town of Bethlehem,
How still we see thee lie,
Above thy deep and dreamless sleep
The silent stars go by.

The music swelled and faded on the night wind. Elin shivered and drew closer to Grandfather. "It's all so pretty it makes me want to cry."

Grandfather's arm tightened across her small shoulders. "It is as if we stand in Bethlehem ourselves," he said softly. "And they are the angels come to sing the new King's birth." Another carol, "Silent Night," began as they edged their way out of the gathering crowd and walked down to the post office corner where a man was selling trees.

"We will have this one," Grandfather decided. "It is short and bushy and the branches more thick than the others." He took one end and Elin the other, and they set off for home again. The voices of the carol singers sounded strangely muffled by the falling snow, until they had passed the radio station on Elgin Street.

The lights from Mr. Kurtsheff's store shone a welcome to them as they rounded Finland Street corner. "I think I better go in and wish Mr. Kurtsheff a merry Christmas for tomorrow, Grandfather." Elin dropped her end of the tree to the ground.

"I think maybe I come, too, Elin, to wish same." Grandfather lowered the trunk of the tree against the steps and knocked the snow from his boots. Mr. Kurtsheff was sitting at the counter, his round eyes fastened upon a little red toy truck, running down the counter at full speed. He put out his pudgy hand to stop it as Elin and Grandfather stamped in the door.

"Mine goodness!" he cried. "Merry Christmas, I'm sure! Just look and see vat old Kurtsheff has got for his tree, please!" He lifted up the truck and chortled with delight. "Whiz bang she go, fast like the real thing. Just watch and I do it again."

They stood while he wound the spring and placed it on the counter. With a leap it was off, buzzing round and round the shining surface like a little red bug. "That's for my little boy nephew. But I'm liking that, too." Mr. Kurtsheff put it reluctantly down on the counter. "But now I must put it away and wrap for the Christmas tree."

"I think it's wonderful, Mr. Kurtsheff." Elin picked up the truck and ran the tiny wheels over the palm of her hand. "Grandfather and I just came in to wish you a merry Christmas."

"We have just buy the tree, Mr. Kurtsheff, and must be on way home. Merry Christmas!" Grandfather offered his hand and Mr. Kurtsheff wiped his on his apron before he took it.

"Vell, I'm sure. Merry Christmas! Now, Elin, let me see. I'm having something for you." He lumbered off toward the candy counter and came back with a green box tied with red ribbon. "Here is for your tree, Elin. Something sweet for you and Juhani."

"Oh, Mr. Kurtsheff, it's so pretty I'll never want to untie it!" Elin admired the big red bow.

"Open it! Open it! Is for the Christmas tree anyway. So open!"

Elin untied the ribbon carefully and looked inside. There were eight candy canes lying together, glistening with their red and white stripes like eight miniature barber's poles.

"Thank you very much, Mr. Kurtsheff. We never had any of these before. I can hang them all on the Christmas tree." She lifted the box to sniff the peppermint fragrance.

The candy canes did look wonderful on the Christmas tree, and so did the Finnish cookies Äiti made specially for it. There were some in the shape of bears, some like reindeer, and even some twisted to the shape of elephants. They had just finished stringing the last one to the spruce needles when a sharp knock sounded at the door. Äiti ran to open it, and in a whirl of snow and wind Anna stepped in on the kitchen mat.

"Anna, where are you going?" Elin stared at her, unbelievingly. "It's getting late."

"Pop brought me round in the car." Anna peeked out from her snow-spangled green hood like a little, round-faced goblin. "I have a present for you to put on the tree."

"A present? Oh, Anna, what is it?" Elin took the small

red and white parcel in her hands, wonderingly.

"I'm not telling. But it's got something to do with ice and it's not very big."

"Do not forget, Elin, what you have, too!" Grandfather called from his chair by the stove.

"Oh, I almost forgot." Elin skipped up the stairs two at a time and brought the small box in its plain white paper wrappings. "I was going to bring it over to you tomorrow morning. It's green and really pretty. It's silk, too!"

"I didn't know you were going to give me a present!" Anna grinned. "But thanks a lot, anyway." She moved toward the door. "I guess I better go now. Pop said not to be too long or the car would freeze up. Merry Christmas!"

"Merry Christmas, Anna! Merry Christmas!" They all shouted after her as she plunged out into the snow.

Elin took the little gift and placed it carefully on one of the lower branches of the tree. Grandfather smiled at her from his corner. Then suddenly he slipped quietly out of the room. He was back in a moment, an old brown sock in his hand. "Now!" he called. "Where is this I hang the sock for Santa Claus, please?"

"Oh, Grandfather!" Elin was astonished. "I didn't know you were going to hang your stocking up, too."

"And why not, please? Grandfather has been good boy I think, and this is fine, good sock."

Elin dragged him, laughing, to the glittering tree. "I hung mine from a lower branch. You hang yours up high."

Then it was time for bed and Christmas Eve was over.

16

The Wonderful
Christmas Gift

"Elin! Elin! Time to be up if we shall be to church on right time, please!" Elin tumbled to the floor and groped for her clothes in the half light of early morning. It was Christmas Day! Outside her window was a world of whirling snow, with the wind shouting, "Merry Christmas!" as it swept down Finland Street.

Christmas Day! It had come at last! Elin shivered as she pulled her green dress on over her head and scampered down the stairs. She was almost through the narrow door of the small living-room where the tree stood, when Isä caught her by the arm.

"Remember, Elin," he cautioned, "we have no Christmas tree until after the Church. Come now, into the hood and the coat, and we shall be on the way."

Grandfather helped her into her clothes, and in the dim light of the morning snow, they hastened on the road to the little Finnish Lutheran church that stood above the town on a mound of rock. Juhani crowed with laughter from Isä's shoulder as the snowflakes settled on his little nose.

All through the joyous singing of the carols and the

great, rolling chords of "Jumala Ompi Linnamme, A mighty fortress is our God," Elin tried very hard to keep her eyes on the book and her heart in the song, but her thoughts wandered back to the splendid tree in the living-room at home.

Then they were on their way back, bracing them-selves against the blizzard, and laughing and calling to all their good friends who passed them on the way.

Once inside the door, Elin whipped off her coat and hood and looked expectantly at Isä. "May I now, please?" She peeped around the corner at the beautiful tree.

Isä nodded. "I think we all see what Santa bring now, shall we?"

"Look what's in my stocking!" Elin pulled out apples and oranges and nuts. Why, there were even some of the cookies Äiti had made the day before, only these were cut in the shape of a rabbit with two long ears and a pink sugar eye.

"What did I say then?" Grandfather shouted from the other side of the tree. "See? My sock is full, too!" So it was! Filled to the brim like Elin's with nuts and candy and fruit. Grandfather emptied them on a piece of tissue paper on the floor. Elin watched, tingling with excite-ment. At the very bottom a little parcel of red paper fell with a thud on the floor.

Grandfather picked it up. "This is heavy." He un-wound the green string and found a piece of rock inside the wrappings. He felt it curiously.

"That's for you, Grandfather," Elin shouted. "From me! It's a piece of rock from the mine where Isä works. I asked Isä to bring it up so I could give it to you. It's a piece of Sudbury for Christmas, to keep with you always. Do you like it?"

Grandfather turned the stone over and over. The veins in it sparkled in the light. "I think there is nothing I rather have for Christmas, Elin, than a piece of Sudbury to carry always." He leaned over and kissed her on the cheek.

Then there was such a mad scramble of paper and wrappings and ribbon that Elin almost burst with excitement.

"Look! Look what Äiti have!" Äiti was sitting on the floor, waving a box. Inside was a pair of cosy blue moccasins trimmed with white fur. Elin was tearing at the red and white paper around the little parcel Anna had left. She lifted the lid of the box. Lying on a bed of soft white batten was a pair of tiny silver skates, fashioned into a brooch! Suddenly she remembered the night she and Grandfather had met Anna in Kresge's. "Now I know why she acted so funny, Grandfather. Look! Anna was buying the brooch at Kresge's and didn't want me to know."

Elin passed the brooch around for them all to see. Juhani was wading through the red, white and green paper wrappings clutching a blue teddy bear to his grey woollen suit. "Look, Juhani! You see, too?" Juhani reached a dimpled hand for it but Elin laughed and snatched it away and pinned it on her dress.

Grandfather was smiling from his chair beside them. "I see now I have very warm feet, Miina. You are good daughter to knit these for me." He held up a pair of heavy dark red woollen socks. Elin did a little jig on the floor in the sturdy new brown shoes she had just taken from the bright red box.

"And me, I got the new brown shirt." Isä held it up with a pleased smile. " 'To my Lemmin with much love and kisses from Miina,' " he read on the card.

But Elin was once again prancing before them, this time in a blue sweater coat with white buttons marching up the front, like a row of tiny daisies through a field of cornflowers.

"Time we had breakfast!" Äiti was gathering up the paper with one hand and her gifts with the other. "I am hungry from the cold and the fun. So food is good for us now. All up! Elin! Lemmin! Juhani! Clear all papers and let us eat! Isä, will you help me please to carry out the boxes!" Grandfather stepped quickly to her side and took some of the load from her arms.

"Äiti!" They both turned around as Elin gave another excited shriek. "There's another one under all these papers. I didn't see it before. Look!"

Everybody looked at the funny, oblong parcel that she pulled from beneath the mound of tissue paper. It was wrapped with green paper and tied with a huge red bow. Elin leaned over and read the tiny card attached. " 'For my little Elin, from Grandfather and Finland.' It's the prettiest parcel of all," she cried.

"Open up this parcel then. I wonder what it can be?" Grandfather said.

She would never get the ribbon undone. Her fingers were all thumbs. She didn't want to cut the silk. It was such a lovely colour for a hair bow. At last the wrapping was off. "It's a box and it's heavy!" She held her breath while she took the lid off. "Skates!" she shouted. Grandfather was seated again with Juhani on his knee, watching her. "Figure skates, Grandfather! These aren't really for me, are they? Not for *keeps?*"

"All for you, little one, for the keeps." Grandfather was just as excited as Elin. "For you from Suomi. Now we shall see if Elin can do the skate, eh? So it must be with girl who help others with the money."

Elin looked up in surprise. Grandfather smiled with pride. "Yes, Äiti and Isä have told me of the work and the money and the bank."

Elin pulled out the figure skates, one at a time. She ran her hand over their smooth, gleaming surface. She put one shoe to her cheek and rubbed it gently over her skin. The leather was soft as silk! Then she rushed at Grandfather and flung her arms around his neck. She wanted to cry, but she didn't know why. All she could say was, "Oh, Grandfather! Oh, Grandfather!" And Grandfather understood and held her close, slowly smoothing her long hair with his gentle hand.

After the roast pig, and the mashed turnips baked in the oven with egg and bread crumbs that was Christmas dinner, the hedelmä soppaa, the sweet dish of apricots, plums and raisins — after all the merriment of the day, Elin was ready for bed.

She awoke in the middle of the night. It had stopped snowing. The moon peered in through the bedroom window. He laid his long, pale fingers across the blanket of her bed, as if he groped for something in the darkness. *The skates!* She remembered now. There had been a pair of figure skates. Had she dreamed they were hers? She was wide awake now, and she crept out of bed softly so that no one would hear. The floor was ice cold under her feet as she tiptoed over to the bureau. There they were, lying together and glistening like snow in the light of the moon! She carried them back to bed and put them on the pillow beside her. With one hand clutching the cool, shining blades, she fell asleep.

17

Skating Lessons are Fun

"Grandfather! Grandfather! Are you ready to go?" Elin hung her schoolbag on the knob of the kitchen door. "Today is the day, isn't it?"

"Home from school already?" Grandfather was pulling on his boots by the kitchen stove. "You sure all the snow swept from the skating place on the lake, Elin?"

"I'm sure as sure. Stepan told me. He's been playing hockey down there with the boys." Elin pulled Grandfather's jacket from the hook behind the door and tried to hurry him into it. "I just can't wait to start skating."

"Please hurry, Grandfather! We'll never get there." Grandfather's steps were long and slow and sure, but Elin tugged at his mittened hand to make him hasten along the path. Most of the rocks were changed into white humps like the loaves of bread Äiti shaped from the dough. Elin carried her skates tucked carefully underneath her arm. When they came to the old log beside the clear patch of ice, she sat down.

Grandfather knelt at her feet. "I undo the buckle of the overshoe, little one."

"Your hands will be cold, Grandfather." Elin tried to

help him by bending down to the other galosh. "I'll unbuckle this one for you!"

Grandfather shook his head with a smile. "Grandfather's hands are often in the cold in Suomi. Many year he has take the shoe from the foot and put on the skate." He put her shoes inside her galoshes again, and placed them in a sheltered spot behind the log, where they crouched like two little brown rabbits.

"Now we shall put on the famous skate, eh, Elin? Right one first, thank you." He pulled the skate on carefully and began to lace it. "Now first of all things with the skate, little one," Grandfather stopped for a moment to look up at Elin, the lace held tightly in his hand "first of all things we learn the way to put the lace in the skate. Like so! See?" He pulled the lace through each hole in the skating-boot, crossing it over her foot. "Now, when we come to last hole we pull, oh so tight, almost till it hurt." And Grandfather tugged until Elin thought the lace would break.

"What are those little hooks for at the top, Grandfather?" Elin pointed to six silver hooks at the top of the skate.

"We shall see." Grandfather went on lacing. "Only wait and we shall see. Now we take this lace and cross it in one knot, like so. And then we have come to the little silver hooks. Behind these the laces go, too, behind each one. So we have come to the top of the skate and we finish with a good strong bow and tuck inside."

"I think I can remember all that, Grandfather. May I try the other one, please?"

"You try this one and Grandfather stand by to help. That is the way. Oh, but more tight, more tight, Elin!" He took the lace from her hands and gave it a strong tug.

"There then is the lace, and now the knot."

"Then around these little silver hooks, and then the strong bow at the top. See, Grandfather? I finished it all by myself."

"We are ready to begin," Grandfather nodded. "The ice, it is yours, Elin. How you go down on these skates?"

"I'm going to try to get to the ice sitting down." Elin started to slither down across the snow.

"Oh, no, little one!" Grandfather's loud laugh rang out across the bare birch trees and the silence of the snow-bound lake. "That is bad. Up again now. Up again and standing on the tips of the toes. That is better. Now down to the ice that way."

Elin tiptoed slowly and carefully down to the shore. She would show Grandfather how well she could skate! One moment now . . . and swish! She was away! But no . . . she wasn't! She was lying face downward on the ice. She pulled herself up, ashamed. Now Grandfather would think she could never learn to be a figure skater.

"There is not the need for the unhappy look, Elin." Grandfather came out on the ice to see that she was not hurt. "That is one thing all those do who have the figure skate on for the first time. Now we shall see the reason why that is. Then we shall not do it again." He motioned her over to the side of the rink, where the crusted snow was piled high in a rolling bank, like a great castle wall.

"Sit down there, little one, on the snow. That is right. Now let us have the look at this skate that make our Elin fall like the sick bird." Grandfather lifted her right foot and ran his hand along the shining steel blade. "Now see why you fall? See how this blade is made like the rocker chair in the kitchen on Finland Street? It is curved, just so little, like the wing of the swallow, so you cannot run on that like you do on the old skate."

"Then how can I stand up, Grandfather?" Elin was discouraged. "I don't see how I can stand up if the skates are going to rock me like a rocking chair."

"You will stand up by putting the weight of the body on the back of the skate, on the heel there." Grandfather put her foot down and drew her to her feet. "See now? That is much better." He gave her a little push then and she skimmed across the ice, holding herself stiffly, so that the weight of her body was resting on her heels.

"I can do it, Grandfather!" She turned a little to swing back to him beside the snowbank. "Look at me! I can do it!"

"Of course, you do it, Elin. That is not hard for the little one who has been on the skate before. Now for the few minutes we shall see you become friends with the new skates. Go out now and do the little skate on the ice." Grandfather gave her a gentle push out on the ice again, and for a moment she glided cautiously around the rink, getting the feel of the magic blades with their strange, nicked toes.

"Elin! Elin!" Grandfather called to her from the snowbank. She skated back to him slowly. "Now we are ready to begin the figure skate."

"Am I going to learn how to lift my leg high in the air and go along on one foot like Anna and Yolande and Wendy, Grandfather?"

"Oh, no, Elin. Not until we learn the things that come at the bottom of all figure skate. And that is the edge, little one."

Elin waited patiently while he paused to find words to explain. "The edge mean that you glide out on the ice on the edge of the skate. First we shall have what is call the inside edge. Now come, put this right foot in front of the left, like as if it make the letter T. Then you will bend the right knee already to push off. Now from there you do the slow glide on the right foot and make one whole circle. Then you change to left foot and make another whole circle. That will make a number. When you do that you will tell me what is that number." Grandfather took her head and turned it gently until it pointed out along her left shoulder and arm. "For this you will hold the head looking out along the left arm and swing both the arms, too. It is the head and the body that will guide the moving, Elin, in this skate; the leg and the foot will follow. Now we are ready, little one. You will begin."

Elin placed her feet as Grandfather had told her and began to skate slowly out on the ice, first in the circle on one foot and then on the other. "It's an eight, Grandfather!" she shouted as she swung back toward him. "I'm making an eight!"

"That is good, little one. That is very good!" Grandfather clapped his mittened hands and bent down to kiss her cold, round cheek. "Oh, we are going to make fine girl for the skating from Elin Laukka. She has the blood for the skate. Now again and again you do that."

Elin glided out again. "Is it all right, Grandfather?" she called. "Do I look all right?"

"For now, Elin, you look like the puppet of wood that jump on the string. But that is no matter. In few days you do that as if you do it all your life, from when you are little girl. Then you feel and look like wooden puppet no more."

It was starting to get dark. "It must be nearly supper-time, Grandfather," Elin reminded him.

"And the first lesson must be over. But you will be

good." Grandfather helped her off with her skates as she sat down on the old log by the shore. "It will take the time and the big heart, but we shall do it, shall we not, little one?" He patted the small red cheek under the snow-hood. Then he took her hand in his and they set off up the snow track, walking quickly to keep warm.

"Can we do it again tomorrow, Grandfather?"

"Tomorrow and the next tomorrow and the next, till you are clever as Grandfather once was on the skate."

"Oh, I'll never be that good, Grandfather! Why, you were a famous skater in Finland. I could never be famous."

"It is not the famous we seek, Elin," Grandfather assured her. "It is for you to be happy on the figure skate. If you do good and please yourself and make others pleased, too, then the rest come in time."

The winter dusk was gathering around them as they took a short cut across the snowbound rocks. The crimson slag flared suddenly in the sky to the west. "Grandfather, do you remember something you told me you'd tell me once, and you never did?" Elin took big, running steps to try to keep up to him.

"Now what is it Grandfather did not do? That is bad thing, is it not? To say a thing will be done and to do it not?"

"Well, remember when I was telling you about the sleeping giant painting the sky? You told me you'd tell me about the night of the midnight sun in Finland. Remember?"

"I did, and I shall do it, too." Grandfather began his story as they hurried on up the main street toward home. "It all happen once in the year in the land of Suomi. That is the night when the sun does not go to bed at all. He stay above the earth for the night long, and this is a night in June. Because this is special night, all the boys and girls of Finland stay up to make the fun, just like at Christmas."

"It must be wonderful to have two Christmases a year."

"Yes, this is like Christmas in summer, true." Grandfather kicked a lump of snow from the sidewalk. "Before the evening begin, everyone go into the sweet-smelling forest to bring back the birch trees to make the leaf houses. In these houses all the good folk of Suomi sit the long day that is really night. They sing loud and merry, and eat the special pancakes, and drink the special drink that is called limonaatia. Every Finnish mother make these thing for that night special."

"And the sun really stays up all night long, Grandfather? *All* night long?"

"It is like here, Elin, almost. They tell me when I come here, that the day in the north country is long, more long in summer than in the south. Is that not so? Yes?"

"I never was down south in Toronto, but that's what the teacher says, so it must be true." Elin pulled her scarf up over her chin. "And they really just sit there all night in those leaf houses and eat? My goodness! They must be terribly full by the time it's morning, mustn't they?"

"No." Grandfather rubbed his ears with his mittens, to feel if they were cold. "They have the music, too, and they dance the folk dance of Finland on the grass, all in the folk costume. You have seen the folk costume, Elin?"

"Chrissie, the girl who takes figure skating with Anna, has one, but I haven't. Chrissie's father and mother came from Czechoslovakia. I guess Äiti forgot to bring one with her when she came here."

"The folk costume are so gay and pretty," Grand-father continued. "And all the little girl like you love very much to wear them. Then there are, too, the fires to look after."

"What fires, Grandfather?"

"At midnight the big fires are light all over the country and kept to burn till morning time. It is around these, then, that the people dance and sing. The men must gather wood to keep the fire light, and the children help. So you see they do not sit the night through."

"I wish I was a little girl in Finland." Elin turned with Grandfather down Finland Street. "I think it would be more fun than Sudbury."

"Every country has the fun, as you call it, little one, in the own way. I think you are lucky to be little girl in Canada."

"Grandfather, there's Anna and Wendy!" Elin pointed to two figures bundled in snowsuits, looming up out of the twilight. "And they've got their skates with them, too! Hi, Anna! Hi, Wendy! Been for your lesson?"

"Hi, Elin!" Wendy raced up the street with Anna at her heels. "You didn't ought to be out so late alone." She stopped quite suddenly as Grandfather stepped out of the shadows. "Oh, I didn't know there was someone with you!"

"It's my Grandfather, Wendy. He came all the way from Finland."

"Oh, hello, Grandfather." Wendy stared at him criti-cally over the tops of her spectacles. "Say, my Dad says our folks came all the way from Ireland once, too. Ireland must be just as far away as Finland."

"It is as far, almost," Grandfather smiled.

"Where've you been, Elin?" Anna elbowed Wendy to

one side to stand in front of Grandfather.

"Skating down at the lake." There was great pride in Elin's voice. "The skates Grandfather gave me are wonderful, too."

"Golly, they're even nicer than mine." Anna ran her hand over the soft, smooth leather.

"Well, you ought to be taking lessons from Mr. Crane now you got skates, Elin." Wendy pushed Anna to the edge of the sidewalk again.

"Grandfather's teaching me to skate, Wendy. So maybe one day I'll be as good as you and Anna. I love it, anyway."

"This Mr. Frost bite the ears if we stay to talk, little ones." Grandfather was trying to hide his ears in his big jacket collar. "Grandfather not wear the warm goblin hood like you, Anna and Wendy."

"You better buy a snow-hood then, Grandfather. Then you'd be really warm." Wendy pushed her spectacles up on her nose with her blue mitten. "Come on, Anna. We have to go. G'bye!"

"G'bye, Elin! G'bye, Grandfather!" Anna slipped on the ice as Wendy grabbed her arm, and they raced off together down the street in the darkness.

"Nice little girls." Grandfather climbed the steps of the house with Elin. "Anna's parents are not of this country, no?"

"They came from Poland a long time ago, Grandfather. They have heaps and heaps of money. Anna's lucky."

Grandfather looked very thoughtful and very wise as he opened the door and the warmth and the light from the kitchen shone out to greet them.

18

Why All the Bells Ring

"I feel as if my skates really belong to me now!" Elin and Grandfather tramped slowly home through the dusk after two hours of practice skating on the lake.

"It is good you feel like that, Elin." Grandfather held her mittened hand closely in his own and Elin knew he was pleased by the look on his clean, square face. "Now is nearly the end of January and every day almost, after the school, you skate for Grandfather. That is much skating for the little one."

They plodded on, their snow-boots sounding crunch-crunch on the snow track. "Grandfather, there's the Giant Slag! He's painting again!" Grandfather looked and nodded. "You know," Elin went on, "I almost forgot to tell you what Anna told me yesterday."

"Yes, and what is this, please?"

"Anna said that Mr. Crane was talking to them about how to look after their skates the other day. He said they're made partly from nickel. So you know what I was thinking?"

"Now what does my Elin think?"

"Well, I was thinking maybe some of the nickel Isä dug out of the mine is right in my own skates. So I should thank Isä for my skates, too."

"That is good, Elin, so good. Sudbury have more than one part in the skating of Elin."

"But Grandfather, isn't it almost time now for me to learn how to lift my leg and fly along the ice like a bird? Couldn't we start that soon?"

"I think it is time for the flying like the bird, too, and tomorrow we shall begin with the free skate. You have learn how to do the eight figure and the three figure. Now come the best of all. And do you know, little one, that this flying down the ice has the bird name, too? It is called 'the sparrow.' Then after 'the sparrow' we learn 'the spin.' You know how you hold the arms close to the body and spin around on the skate? You see that, Elin?"

"No, Grandfather. Why, I don't think even Anna and Yolande and Wendy can do that. You mean I'm going to learn it all, Grandfather? Even the things the big people do?"

"You will learn it all, Elin. When the bones are young and strong, that is when one can do the figure skate best. So why not learn it all then? And after that we do 'the spread eagle'."

"Another bird, Grandfather? What's that like?"

"It is where you hold the both skates pointing away from each other so they make a straight line. Like so." Grandfather put his heels together and stood with his feet pointing in opposite directions. "That is little hard to do but you learn fast. My Elin is good skater." He caught her hand in his again and they went on up the path, Elin's thoughts a whirl of sparrows and eagles and leaping on ice.

She ran all the way home from school the next day. Grandfather was waiting for her on the front veranda with her skates on his arm. "Let's hurry, Grandfather!" She tossed her schoolbag in the front door. "Today is terribly important. I know it's going to feel just like a bird!"

"Oh, Grandfather! I'm all out of puff from hurrying!" Elin sat down on the old log for a moment when they arrived at the lake. Only for a moment. Then out she skimmed on the ice, no longer like the wooden puppet Grandfather had called her on the first day, but like the drifting white seagull she wished to be, gliding with grace and dignity across the ice. Then Grandfather took her one leg in his hand and lifted it high behind her body, while she stretched her arms out like two wings.

"Now, Elin, that is the way I shall see you do this sparrow, little one. Now is time to go. Pretend you are the bird now, Elin."

Elin glided up the ice and started to lift her left leg behind her. Down it came with a thump and she had to swing her arms out to stop herself from falling.

"Hold the arms out straight! Like so!" Grandfather held his arms out like wings of an airplane. "Keep the back arch and hold up the head. Then you not fall!"

Elin skimmed off again, a little more quickly this time. Suddenly her left leg was high in the air behind her, her arms were outspread and she was really floating along the ice like a bird! For a moment she was so excited she could not even call to Grandfather. She gave a little skipping hop on the ice as she finished her second sparrow, and spun over into Grandfather's arms. They both fell down, laughing merrily, on the snowbank.

"It does feel like a bird, Grandfather!" Elin hugged his arm. "It's as good as having wings. And it's not too hard either."

"No, it is not hard when you have learn to know your new skates, Elin. But it you feel like the bird now, wait, little one, till you come to the leap on the ice. Then you feel like the lark in the cloud."

"How do I do it, Grandfather? Is it very hard, harder than this?"

"It is not easy, this leap." Grandfather brushed the snow from her coat. "It is made from that figure three you have learn to do on ice. It is the curl in the middle of that figure three. Instead of doing that curl on the ice, you take the big leap and do it in the air."

"And when can I do that, please? Can we start that soon, Grandfather?"

"Wait! Wait, little one!" Grandfather's clear blue eyes twinkled with laughter, and he pulled one of the shining pigtails hanging out over the green coat. "We must be very good at each thing we do. In good time we come to this leap. Only learn what I teach you now and that will come, too."

"We can skate a long time on Saturday." Elin took off her mitten to search for a handkerchief. "We could come down early in the morning and stay all day."

"It is not good to do too much at once, Elin. All in time." Grandfather drew out his big white handkerchief for her. "All in time. But Saturday we perhaps do get the start on this leap, maybe."

Saturday morning Elin jumped out of bed very early and raced to the window, clutching her scanty nightgown closely about her, for the room was very cold. She blew on the frosted window-pane to make a little clear space. The melting frost dribbled to the window-sill. Outside, the world shimmered with sun and snow. A wonderful day for skating! She hurried into her clothes and was down in the kitchen in a jiffy.

"This is the day for the skate, Elin!" Grandfather was finishing a cup of coffee at the kitchen table. "We hurry now."

"Don't go without me!" Elin gulped her porridge while Grandfather pulled on his coat. "Please wait for me!" she called through a mouthful of oatmeal.

"I go to sniff fresh air." Grandfather set his cap at a jaunty angle. "I be back." He disappeared through the kitchen door. In a moment he was back, rubbing his hands and wrinkling his nose.

"Oh, my! Oh, my!" He held his hands over the stove to warm them. "I do not know it is so cold when the sun shines." He blew out his cheeks.

"Cold? Is it very cold out?" Elin ran to the window. "I'll see what the temperature is." She puffed out her cheeks like tiny pink balloons, and peered out through the little clear space to the thermometer hanging outside. "Grandfather! Grandfather, come and look! It's thirty below zero!"

"Thirty below the zero!" Grandfather leaned his cheek close to Elin's to peer out, too. "It is not strange then, that old Grandfather is feel the cold. Thirty below the zero! Whew!"

Elin looked at Grandfather. Grandfather looked at Elin. Suddenly Elin began to giggle. Grandfather roared with laughter. "I guess today we skate on kitchen floor, where Grandfather can sit and teach by kitchen stove! This old sun, he is fool Grandfather for the first time!"

There were other days like that Saturday, days when Elin couldn't skate, when the frost rimed the coat collars and the hair with a spray of diamonds. "You have to walk fast now, if you go out in this," Elin warned Grandfather. "Or you'll just freeze."

Then there were days of snow when Sudbury was dark with a shouting blizzard and Elin groped her way home from school, knowing there would be no skating on the lake for some time. It would take Stepan and his friends almost a week to pile the snow back on the lakeshore in great scoops, like the ice cream Elin used to pile on the crusty cones in Mr. Kurtsheff's store.

But as soon as there was space enough for even a tiny sparrow, Elin and Grandfather would be back again, and Elin became more and more sure of her flying leaps down the ice, and did her steps with ease and poise.

"I'm so tired, Grandfather," she would sigh sometimes. "Do we have to go today?"

"Elin, only when one work hard do one get the thing he want most." And Grandfather would take her hand and set off for the lake. "Come now, little one."

"All right, Grandfather. It's only now I'm tired. When I'm down there skating I don't feel tired at all."

One day near the end of February, Elin was sliding on the patch of clear ice in the schoolyard at recess. "Hey, Elin!" It was Anna. Wendy and Yolande were close behind. "Do you want to know something awfully nice and awfully exciting?"

Elin nodded.

"Well, Mr. Crane says we can be in the Carnival this year. Isn't that wonderful?"

"And I'm going to be Champlain, Samuel *de* Champlain," Wendy swaggered. "I don't know what the *de* stands for, but it's sure a smart name!"

"You mean you're going to skate in front of all those people in the arena?"

"That's right." Anna gave a little skip of joy. "And so's Yolande and so's Elizabeth and so's Chrissie."

"I wish you could be in it, too, Elin," Yolande said, politely. "I'm sorry you couldn't take lessons with us."

"You should have taken lessons when you had the money." Wendy wiped her spectacles on the sleeve of her coat. "You might even have been one of my explorer men."

"You're lucky," was all Elin said.

Later, in the arithmetic class, an idea came to Elin. She was trying to do a sum, but the picture of Anna, Yolande and Wendy skimming down the ice in lovely costumes, kept creeping over the page. Then quite suddenly she thought, *But why couldn't I do it, too? I can skate as well as Anna and perhaps, if I asked and was specially good, Mr. Crane might let me skate with them!*

"Elin! Elin! The teacher's asking you a question!" Stepan pulled one of her pigtails to make her answer.

"Yes, Miss Jenkinson!" Elin stumbled to her feet and stammered an answer.

It was the same in geography class. They were studying the people and customs of South America. *That looks just like costumes for a carnival,* she thought, gazing at the vivid, coloured pictures the teacher was showing them. *The boys and girls in South America must feel as if they're in a carnival all the time.* How exciting it would be to put on a real costume and skate before a real audience. Maybe it wasn't right to ask Mr. Crane, though. Maybe she shouldn't do it today. Tomorrow might be a better day. But Mr. Crane was so nice. He had been so friendly on that day long ago when he had said she could go in the Carnival if she took lessons. Well, she had taken lessons, hadn't she? And from Grandfather, who used to be a *champion* skater once upon a time.

I'll find out from Anna when I should go to see Mr. Crane about it, she thought.

But Anna left school earlier than Elin, who had one arithmetic sum to correct because of her daydreaming. She snatched her coat and hat from the hook as soon as she had handed her paper to the teacher, and struggled into her galoshes. She left the buckles undone in her haste to catch up to Anna, Yolande and Wendy. She could see them far ahead, loitering here and there to slide on the clear patches of ice by the side of the road. When she caught up to them she was so out of breath she could hardly speak.

"Hello, Elin!" Anna threw her arm around Elin's shoulders. "Get your arithmetic all right?"

"Yes, it wasn't hard. I'd only made a mistake copying it down," Elin puffed. She bent down to fasten her galoshes.

"I'd have waited for you, Elin, but I'm supposed to be home early today to help get supper. Mom and Pop are going out to a concert at Polish Hall tonight." Anna held Elin's school-bag for her.

"Anna!" Elin stood up, pulled down her coat and fixed her hood straight on her head. "Anna, I want to ask you something."

"Well, what do you want to ask me?"

"I bet she's got a secret! I bet she's got a secret!" Wendy came back from the slide where she had been coasting. "Tell me, too."

"If it's a secret we aren't supposed to listen, Wendy,"

Yolande reminded her. "Maybe Elin doesn't want us to hear."

"Oh, yes!" Elin began to walk on with them slowly. "You can hear. Anna, you know Grandfather has been teaching me to figure skate like you. Well . . . " She hesitated. "Well, do you suppose Mr. Crane would let me go in the Carnival with you, maybe?"

"My goodness, Elin!" Wendy laughed very loud. "Don't you know it's only people like us that pay for lessons that can go in the Carnival? That's what the Carnival's for."

"Oh, be quiet, Wendy." Anna put her arm through Elin's. "You see, Elin, the Carnival's so's our Moms and Pops can see how good we're getting in our lessons, so Mr. Crane says. That's why it's only those that take at the arena that can go in. Maybe next year you'll have some money and can take with us."

"Yes, and we'd be really glad." Yolande slipped her hand through Elin's other arm. "I'd like you to skate beside me if Mr. Crane would let you."

"She'd be better skating beside me," Wendy objected. "She'd learn more. I'm pretty good at it. Next year I'll likely be a king or something like that."

"Don't you think you could take lessons with us next year?" Yolande tried to make Elin smile.

Elin did not answer. At the corner of Finland Street she started to run. She was trying hard not to cry, but the tears spilled over by the time she reached the door. Grandfather was sitting in the kitchen chatting with Äiti. He looked up in astonishment as she rushed past them and upstairs. She flung herself on the bed. In a moment she heard Grandfather's slow step on the stairs. Then he was sitting on the bed beside her.

"And what is the big sorrow that we weep so, little one?" He drew out his big white handkerchief and gently dried her face.

"I wanted to be in the Carnival and they said no!"

"And who is this 'they' that say no, please?"

"Anna and Wendy and Yolande. They're going to skate in the Carnival, and I thought maybe the teacher would let me," she took a deep, sobbing breath, "but Wendy said the Carnival's only for people that pay for lessons!"

"Only if you pay for the lesson you go in." Grandfather frowned. "I see."

"I don't see why you always have to have money to do things." Elin quivered with another sob. "Anna and Wendy and Yolande are lucky. They're rich and they can do what they want."

Grandfather shook her gently and she remembered the cross look he had given her once before when she had said something like that. He waited patiently until all the tears were gone. Then he took her chin firmly in his big hand and turned her face up to his. "Elin, I have something I want much to say to you. Better we say it now. This money you talk of. I want you to see it is of no matter." He wiped a stray tear from her stained cheek. "There can be much happiness without much money. In Finland we have the word for it. *Sisu* it is. That means you have the feeling that the place you are is the right place. And where that place is you must *work* to make it the right place. That is the spirit of the Finn, Elin. That is what make him happy and content. He do not strive after the money, but know it is here and here that count." Grandfather pointed, as he spoke these words, to his head and his heart. "It is not if you

152

have a lot of money and can go in the Carnival."

"Well, but don't some little boys and girls have more money than others in Finland, too, Grandfather?"

"Yes, some little girl and boy have more than the other but that does not count. All wear the same plain clothes to school, and learn that it is the mind, the manners and the heart that make him great in Suomi, not the money. And so it must be here in this new country, Canada. Are you real Finn, Elin, little one?"

"It's hard, Grandfather, but I'll try. Only it wouldn't be so hard trying if I could be in the Carnival!"

"Once, long ago, I hear a little girl say she would be oh, so happy, if only she learn to figure skate."

That's me he means, Elin thought, avoiding Grandfather's keen eyes.

"She thought, she tell me, she would not learn because she have no money. She is give her money to Isä and Äiti." Grandfather playfully pulled one of her long, blonde pigtails. "Now she is not happy forever because she want something more. Yes?"

"I'm sorry, Grandfather. I'll be a real Finn. Anyhow I can skate and lots of people can't." She crinkled the corners of her blue eyes at Grandfather. "Is that better?"

"That is good, very good." Grandfather hugged her close. "You know once, long, long ago, when I was little boy in Finland, I know an old lady, a very old lady. Sometime I think her somebody's fairy godmother. She give me cookies and candy, and live in funny little house in pretty lane. The pines, like what grow on hills here, grow all round her house. She need only to touch the good soil, and the flowers of much beauty spring up."

"Oh." Elin was not much interested in old ladies.

"This old lady say that whenever she see somebody

smile, she hear all the bells ring loud and clear."

"What bells?"

"Why, I think she mean all the bells of fairyland, don't you, little one?"

"Oh, I like that, Grandfather!" Elin clapped her hands. "So every time I smile, or Juhani smiles, or Isä smiles, or Äiti smiles, the bells of fairyland all ring?"

"That is right. Now do we wish that bells ring on Finland Street, the same like they ring in Finland?"

Elin leaned over and hugged him. "We'll make them ring even louder on Finland Street, Grandfather," she said. "And when I'm skating I feel as if I have bells on my toes, too, just like the nursery rhyme says."

19

Carnival Surprises

"It is the weather like Finland now." Grandfather glanced out of the window the following morning. The wind rushed out of the northland, sweeping down Finland Street and across Sudbury in a fury of snow and sound. Elin thought Grandfather seemed a little sad.

"I guess I better bundle up tight in my clothes today, Grandfather, and look fat like a snowman." She tried to make him smile. "It'll be all drifts and snow on the way to school."

The morning wore on slowly. The wind droned continuously through Miss Jenkinson's voice and the lessons, and snow lashed the windows.

"Can I sit with you?" Elin caught Anna's arm when the noon bell rang. "I brought my lunch today. Äiti said it would be too stormy to go home."

"Sure!" Anna smiled, and Elin remembered the secret about the bells ringing and smiled back. "I thought you were mad at us yesterday, Elin. But I'm glad you're not." They squeezed into a place on the bench in the basement lunch room. "I got an idea after you went. Want to know what it is?"

"I'd love to, please."

"We can all ask one person to the Carnival free, and they can have a good seat right near the front." Anna tore the paper from her sandwiches and peeked inside. "Mom and Pop are buying tickets together, anyway, so I thought I'd ask you. Would you like to come?"

"Oh, Anna!" Elin dropped her peanut butter sandwich on the waxed paper. "Could I really come and not have to pay anything?"

"Sure, I told Mom about it and she says it'd be all right. I'll get the ticket as soon as they're ready. Gee, I'm glad you're coming."

"Anybody like to trade a piece of cake for a sandwich?" Elizabeth didn't like sandwiches. "Mine's a plum jelly sandwich!"

"My Mum's plum jelly's better than yours," Wendy shouted down the bench to her. "But I guess I'll trade. Here's a piece of lemon cake."

"What are you wearing in the Carnival, Anna?" Elin forgot to eat her lunch. "And what's Yolande wearing?"

"Say!" Anna took a package from her little yellow lunch box. "Would you like some chocolate cake? Mom gave me two pieces and I'm almost full." She leaned over and laid a piece of rich dark chocolate cake, smothered in a frothy white icing, on Elin's waxed paper.

"Thanks a lot!"

"That's all right." Anna lifted out the other piece. "See? I told you I had two lots, didn't I? What am I going to wear?" she spoke through a mouthful of brown crumbs. "Well, it's really going to be beautiful. The whole thing's called Our Canada. It's supposed to show all the different kinds of people who live in Canada, and where they all came from. So we're all going to wear costumes like the boys and girls wear in the old country."

"You mean folk costumes?" Elin's upper lip wore a moustache of white icing. "Grandfather told me all about how the boys and girls wear the folk costumes for the special days in Finland. They must be so pretty!"

"Mom has one that fitted her when she came here a long, long time ago." Anna wiped her chin with the back of her hand. "But now she's got so fat it doesn't fit her any more. So she's cutting it down to fit me. Gosh, it's pretty, too. I wish I wore it every day."

"What's Yolande wearing?" Elin wanted to know everything!

"Yolande's going to be France, so her Mom got a book from Miss McLean at the Library, to see what the little girls wear in France. She's making Yolande's costume. Chrissie's going to be Czechoslovakia, and she has a costume that just fits."

"Where did she get hers?"

"Her Mom brought it with her from her home. Then there's Elizabeth. She's going to be Canada, I think. She's got an awfully pretty costume, all silver with spangles on it, and a silver crown on her head. And Wendy's Champlain, like she told you."

"Are there any more girls in it?" Elin made her finger into a little pink shovel, scraping up the last little dabs of sticky icing from the waxed paper.

"Oh, yes, lots!" Anna brushed the crumbs from her lap and shook her dark blue skirt. "There's one for all the countries we study almost. And when we come out there'll be lovely lights shining on us, all colours, and they'll change colour while we skate. I bet you'll love it, Elin."

"I know I will," Elin sighed.

In the afternoon the wind ceased. A sudden quiet

came down over the world. "It's all drifts, Elin," Stepan whispered loudly behind his notebook. "Look out of the window." Elin put her finger to her lips. "Aw, who's scared of the teacher? Will you come sleighing on the hill after school, Elin? Some of the kids are going skiing." He ducked down quickly as a loud knock sounded at the schoolroom door. The teacher walked down past him. All the boys and girls slithered round cautiously in their seats to see who it was. Elin could hear Anna and Yolande whispering in front of her.

Miss Jenkinson opened the door but nobody could hear a word she said. "It's a letter," Stepan announced in a dramatic whisper. "I saw her take . . . " He closed his mouth tightly and sat up straight as a ruler when the teacher walked up the aisle to Elin and handed her a note. The whole class stared curiously at Elin. She blushed and laid the note on her desk, unopened. Maybe Äiti wanted her to call in at Mr. Kurtsheff's store on the way home, and had forgotten to tell her. She had done that once before. When the boys and girls in the room had forgotten about her again, and were writing an exercise, Elin took up the note and opened it. "You are to call in at the Skating Club Arena on your way home. Mr. Crane wishes to see you," she read.

Why was her heart knocking so hard under her blue sweater? Why did she suddenly want to cry? She knew what the note meant. Mr. Crane must have heard that she had said only rich people were able to go in the carnival. What would he do to her now? Maybe he would call a policeman and have her put in jail. *Worse still, he might ask her to pay a lot of money to him for saying such things about the Club!*

There! The bell was ringing. There was a noisy

scramble to put away books and papers and pens. How warm and cosy and secure it was here, with the rows of ink-stained desks, and the smell of chalk and rubber boots. Now she would have to go to the arena. Now! *I must try to get away before Stepan asks me what the note said*, she thought.

She flung herself into her coat and snow-hood in the dim cloakroom and did not stop to fasten her galoshes. The metal buckles made an angry, rasping sound as she fled through the snow. If she reached Mr. Crane before Anna and Yolande and the rest arrived for rehearsal, perhaps they would not hear what he had to say to her. The air was cold, but she was hotter than she had ever been before. The little blue sweater with the white buttons that Äiti had made for her smelled strangely from the heat of her body, and she could feel her cheeks burn.

The lights were all on inside the arena and a group of young people were doing twists and turns at the far end of the ice.

Mr. Crane was not there! She could not see him. Perhaps it would be better to go right home. Äiti needed her to look after Juhani. She would come another day. But what had Grandfather said? "Are you real Finn, Elin, little one?" She *must* be a real Finn or Grandfather would be ashamed of her. She would walk carefully along the ice to ask where the teacher was.

There he was! Suddenly he looked up and saw her, coming slowly and fearfully down across the ice floor. He skated out swiftly and swirled to an abrupt stop right in front of her. "Well, young lady, and what can we do for you today?" He bent over slightly to look into her face.

He didn't even remember who she was! She took a

deep breath. "I'm Elin Laukka and I live on Finland Street. I got a note . . . "

"Oh, so you're the young lady we've been waiting for." The jolly young man reached down and took her hands in his. "I remember you now. You came to register and then couldn't take lessons. Come on and we'll put on skates and see what you can do." He led her by the hand over to the bench.

There must be some mistake, Elin thought. *He really didn't hear me or know who I am.* "Mr. Crane, I'm . . ." But he had gone, skimming over the ice to the dressing-rooms. In a moment he was back again with a pair of skates.

"Grandfather brought these down for you this afternoon." He pulled off her galoshes. "He thinks you're a pretty clever little skater, young lady. But you've got to show us. We'll take off . . . "

"But why?" Elin could stand this mystery no longer. "Why am I to wear my skates?"

"You mean you don't know why you're here?" The young man stopped doing up her skates and sat down beside her on the bench.

Elin shook her head and wondered if he could hear her heart thumping.

"Well, my goodness, we'll soon straighten that out. Your grandfather was down here this afternoon. He thinks you're pretty smart on skates, and wants you to have lessons with us next year. So he's going to give them to you. How's that for a start?" Mr. Crane patted her hand as he talked. "And not only that. He'd especially like you to be in the Carnival next month, if you're good enough. He wants to see you skate before he goes back to Finland."

160

At first she was afraid that she would forget all that Grandfather had told her, and disgrace him and Finland; afraid that she would fall, or would not skate with the grace and beauty he had taught her. But then, when she felt the smooth ice beneath her blades, and saw the long stretch of rink before her, she forgot all but the joy of the moment. How long ago it seemed that she was sitting on that very bench, where Mr. Crane now sat watching her, sitting there with a half-eaten bag of candies beside her in the dark, and here she was, taking wings and skimming down the ice like a bird in flight.

Suddenly Mr. Crane sprang up and skated quickly over to her. He took her hand in his and away they went then, together, across the ice floor. Someone in the rear turned off the big lights and threw a spotlight on them and Elin's blue sweater turned to gold, and the world around her to fairyland.

Later, when the dark was falling and she was wading home through the snow twilight with a heart so filled with happiness she thought it would burst, she remembered some of Mr. Crane's words: *before he goes back to Finland*. She stopped quite still in the snow drifts. Grandfather going back to Finland? Why, it wasn't true! She could never be happy without Grandfather now. She loved him more than anyone in the whole, wide world. *Happy?* Grandfather had said something important about that, too. "Now she is not happy forever because she want something more. Yes?" No, she wanted nothing more now. Grandfather would never really go. Mr. Crane had made a mistake about that. So now she had everything she had ever wished for. She was going in the Carnival and Grandfather would see her.

20

Elin Must be Brave

"Grandfather!" Elin saw him clearing snow from the front walk as she raced up Finland Street. "Oh, Grandfather, everything's so wonderful and it's all because of you!"

"And why is this, Elin?" He leaned on his shovel to rest.

"Because of the figure-skating lessons and the Carnival and everything!"

"Figure-skating lessons? What is this I hear? You have been doing the figure skating today and Grandfather not there?"

"But Mr. Crane said it was you who did it. You asked him if I could go in the Carnival, and paid him so I could take lessons next year. Mr. Crane said so!"

"So, maybe it was Grandfather. Maybe so. Maybe it was."

"Grandfather, you're just fooling me!" Elin flung herself upon him. "You know it was you!"

"So, so, little one. What did the teacher think of the figure skating?"

"He says I'm good like you when you were young, and I'm going to be in the Carnival. I'm to be Finland!

Oh, Grandfather, just think! I'm going to be Finland in front of all those people!"

"Just like I want very much, little one. You will be beautiful just like Finland, eh?"

"You know, Grandfather, I can't really believe it. I didn't know I was going to be able to take figure-skating lessons when I gave the money to Isä and Äiti. Now I'm even going to be in the Carnival! Oh, Grandfather, it's so wonderful!"

Grandfather brushed the snow from her coat. "That is because you have learn the Sisu we talk of before, Elin. You learn to be happy with what you have. Then many good things come your way. You are good Finn. You have learned the Sisu." He took her hand and they walked into the warm brightness of the house.

Before he goes back to Finland . . . before he goes back to Finland! The words Mr. Crane had said spun around in Elin's head like the march on the phonograph record at school. But there was Grandfather, his stocking feet up on the fender of the stove, drinking his coffee and chatting gaily in Finnish with Isä and Äiti. He would stay with them forever on Finland Street.

"I have no costume for the Carnival!" Elin remembered suddenly while she was getting ready for bed. "How can I earn enough money to buy stuff to make one?" Perhaps Mr. Kurtsheff would let her work there after school.

She was kneeling down to say her prayers when Grandfather appeared at the door with a brown paper parcel in his hand.

"Perhaps you like to see what is in here, eh?" Grandfather put the parcel in her hands.

Elin tore eagerly at the wrappings. She could hardly

believe what she saw. There, carefully folded inside, was the beautiful costume of the little girl of Finland; the wide, long, many-coloured skirt, the black velvet bodice embroidered in scarlet and gold, and the white blouse. There were big tears in her eyes as she looked at Grandfather.

"That is gift from Finland, Elin." Grandfather held her close. "All the way that come with Grandfather from Suomi, so you do not forget the spirit of the Finn. I want you to wear that with the great pride in the heart when you skate."

"I shall, Grandfather. Oh, I shall!"

"Now is time to go to sleep." Grandfather turned off the light and bent to kiss her. Suddenly, outside, the glow of the slag stole up over the snow hills, sending long shafts of flame into the night. Elin sat up and looked out of the window. "It's like a million candles all burning at once, isn't it, Grandfather?"

"Like a million candles all burn in the darkness. Elin, if some day a person come to you and say you see these million candles no more, would you be sad, little one?"

"Oh, yes, Grandfather, I would."

"That is the way it is with Grandfather. Only Grandfather be terribly sad if he never again see the midnight sun."

"Are you going away, Grandfather?" Elin tried to stop the tears spilling down her face.

Grandfather drew his big white handkerchief from his pocket and held it up to her nose. "Blow now," he said. "Big blow and then we hear the bells ring again!"

She must keep the bells ringing on Finland Street! She tried to smile.

"After the Carnival and my Elin skate, I go to the

homeland. It is like the big ache here." He pointed to his heart. "It is like the big, big ache to see the fields of wheat, that shine in the sun like my Elin's hair, and the green woods of spruce tree and birch tree and pine on the edge of the field. It is big loneliness for these and for the home. And then there is my pony. Who look after him and my cows and all my little pigs if I do not go back to Suomi. Who, eh?"

"Have you got a pony in Finland, Grandfather?"

"Oh, yes, little one. His name is Tähti. That mean 'Star' in English. He pull my sleigh for me in winter. Now the good neighbours look after Tähti and my farm for me. But not for long. They wait for me to come back to Suomi again."

"I could go back to Suomi, Grandfather, and see Tähti and everything!"

"Now how you go back to place you never been, Elin?" Grandfather pulled her pink ear. "You never been yet to good Suomi. It is Grandfather who go back and Elin stay here in Canada."

"But I'd like a pony. I'd like Finland just as much as Canada."

"No." Grandfather shook his head wisely. "You would not see these million candles in the darkness again and you would be lonely. No, Elin. Every man has his home, and for now this is yours. And you must make your country great and happy country in your lifetime, like we make Finland great and happy. You must be strong like the rock, and gay and of much beauty like the birch tree that cling to it. And you will keep the spirit of the Finn with you always. See?" He pointed. "Our Giant Slag come again!"

Out of the darkness the glow leaped once more, like

a great sun, rising swiftly and strangely in the west. The fierce Giant Slag was painting the sky, sending his shafts of flame into the night. Elin and Grandfather watched until the last faint glimmer slipped down behind the Giant's mighty body, and the world was once again snow and darkness.

21

The Dress Rehearsal

"I'm scared, Anna. What if I don't do what Grandfather told me?" Elin shifted nervously from one foot to the other as they waited at the entrance to the rink.

"You needn't worry, Elin." Anna squeezed her hand. "This is only the first time you've been here to rehearsal. You should have seen all the mistakes we made the first day. It was awful."

"But I don't want to make mistakes." Elin frowned. "What would Grandfather say? He told me I must not be just good. I must be perfect."

"Gosh! It must be hard to be perfect. Look!" Anna pointed to the door. "There goes Chrissie and you're after her. Mr. Crane's calling you."

"All right, Finland! Your turn next, please! Follow Czechoslovakia there, please!"

Elin skimmed out and a great silence fell over the rink. Only the soft singing of the blades as they cut into the smooth ice, and the loud beating of her heart! Out of the corner of her eye she could see the girls in their places on the ice watching her dance over the ice. Anna was smiling and so was Mr. Crane . . . and Wendy . . . Wendy was grinning from ear to ear, peering at her over the top of her horn-rimmed spectacles.

Suddenly Elin knew. Only the skating mattered. Only curving edges and the difficult spread eagles; the graceful sparrows, when the leg was lifted like a gull's wing in the air; the dizzy spins, when she held her arms close to her body, and whirled round and round on her toes like a toy top. And then it was time for her leap and half turn and the jump, and the sudden sailing down the ice on the last sparrow, the coming to a halt and the swift curtsey. Elin's part in her first rehearsal was done.

For a moment the girls waited, silent. It was Wendy who began to clap. Then the whole arena was filled with clapping. "Elin, it was wonderful! Oh, Elin, you're so good!" they shouted. Mr. Crane was balancing on his skates, patiently waiting to go on, smiling at her across the shining ice.

The next night was the dress rehearsal. Elin took her Finnish costume from its brown-paper wrappings and carried it with her to the arena. It was a long rehearsal.

"I hope you will remember all that I have told you!" Mr. Crane called to them when it was over. "Go home now and get a good supper. Have a long night's rest and be back here early tomorrow night. Do as your dressers and make-up artists tell you, too." He turned to go, shouting back over his shoulder, "Good luck to you! And give Sudbury the best skating carnival it will ever have!"

Grandfather was waiting for Elin at the door. "So, little one, the night is almost come, then." He helped her take off her galoshes and coat and put them behind the stove to dry. "And how is it go, this last night before we are famous skater? How is it go, eh?"

Elin yawned sleepily and sat down on the floor,

leaning her head on Grandfather's knee. "You know, Grandfather, sometimes I wish tomorrow night wouldn't ever come. Ever!"

"Is it because you have the fun and the happiness while you skate, little one, and never want to stop?"

Elin nodded. "Grandfather, when something really nice happens, why does it have to go so fast?"

"Elin, tomorrow night is just the start of something nice. Just the beginning of something that grow big and more big as the year go by."

Elin was silent.

"You know not what I try to say, little one," Grandfather went on slowly. "It is this. Tomorrow night you will be Finland. Perhaps never again you be Finland. Oh, yes, Elin, you will skate more and more. Perhaps one day you be great skater. When one has the figure skating in the heart and mind like my Elin, she does not stop where she just begin." He paused for a moment, his hand on her head.

"You really think one day I might be a champion skater, Grandfather? A real *champion?*"

"I think so, Elin. And do you know what other thing may happen?" Grandfather caught her chin in his broad palm and turned her face to his. "Some day you may come to Suomi, to skate before all the people in the good Finland. And then you skate not as Finland any more, but as Miss Canada. How you like that?"

"Grandfather, that sounds just too good to be true," Elin sighed. "I'd be skating for Canada, just like you skated for Finland, and you'd be there, too, to see me."

Grandfather looked over her head to the darkness beyond the window. "Yes, little one, I shall be there. But it is no matter how great you be as a skater, Elin. Tomorrow night will be the happiest skate you ever do, this first skating when you are Finland. And as the year go by, you will find this Carnival is not like something you leave behind, little one. Oh no! It is something you carry with you. Every year it will mean more of happiness for you when you look back on it far away. This Carnival is something you win alone, Elin."

"But I didn't win the Carnival, Grandfather. It was all you. You gave me the skates and the lessons, and asked Mr. Crane."

"No, I think not so." Grandfather shook his head slowly. "It was you, Elin. You have give up the skating lessons so Äiti and Isä be happy again. You give up this money you save. So there is reason why you be happier than any on this night of the Carnival. You win the Carnival for your own by being strong, fine Finn."

"Mr. Crane says we're not really Finns or Czechs or Poles or anything like that any more, Grandfather. He says we're Canadians, every one. It's just the same in the United States, too. The people there have come from all over the world, but when they live in the United States, they're Americans. That's what the teacher says, too."

"And this Mr. Crane and the teacher, they are right, Elin. And do you know something else? It is not even to be Canadian, or American, or Finnish, or Polish like Anna, or Czechoslovakian like Chrissie that matter at all. It is the *kind* of person you are, and if you are good, kind and true person. Then you will help your country to be good, kind and true, too."

"But it's fun that Isä and Äiti came from Finland, Grandfather, even if I am a Canadian. Isn't it good to be glad of that?"

"Yes, Elin. It is good to remember sometime the fine

thing the Finnish blood give you. For you it has given the Sisu. My Elin know her right place and is happy in it. But come. There is big, big day tomorrow and for the big day we must have the big sleep. Off to bed, Elin!"

Elin scrambled to her feet and stretched a little. "Good night, Grandfather!" She kissed him and went slowly upstairs to bed, thinking over the words Grandfather had spoken. *It must be true*, she thought. *Grandfather is wiser than anyone in the whole, wide world, even wiser than Isä or Äiti, or Miss Jenkinson, the teacher.*

Elin didn't know quite why. It was all a little hard to understand. But Grandfather had said it, and it would come true.

22

"Some Day You Skate For Canada"

There's something special about today. What is it? Elin opened her eyes and lay there thinking. Then she heard the March wind blustering at the window. "It's the day of the Carnival!" she remembered, leaping out of bed. "Today I'm not Elin Laukka. I'm Finland!"

Will it ever be four o' clock! Elin thought, as the hours of school dragged on wearily. But at last the bell rang and she ran to the cloakroom with Anna to put on coat and galoshes.

"I still have to polish my skates." Anna grunted from bending to fasten the buckles.

"I do, too." Elin pulled on her snow-hood. "Grandfather gave me some money to buy some white stuff with. See?" She held up a little brown paper wad, hidden in the folds of her mitten.

"Let's go now then. You'll have to go down to the drug store to buy the cleaning stuff, so you can come part way home with me." Anna took her hand and they ran out into the snow.

The wind blew little drifts across the sidewalk and they slithered along, for there was a thin coating of ice underneath the snow.

"Is Mr. Kurtsheff coming to see you skate, Elin?" Anna slid past the little grocery store.

"He said he wouldn't miss it for anything. And do you know what?"

"No, what?"

"Mr. Kurtsheff is taking Stepan, too, because he didn't have enough money to buy a ticket. Isn't that fun?"

"Wonderful!" Anna shook the wet snow from her scarf and face. "Which drug store are you going to?"

"We'll go to Rath's." Elin took a long slide on a piece of bare ice. "That's the nearest."

At the next corner there was a large sign swinging and creaking in the wind. "Rath's Drug Store. We serve the sick well." Going in they almost knocked down a fat lady on the way out with her arms full of bundles.

"Please excuse me," Elin said. "I didn't mean it."

"Gosh, I'm awful sorry." Anna picked up one of the bundles and handed it to the lady.

"Well, young lady, what can I do for you?"

"I'll have a bottle of shoe-white, please." Elin looked up at the young man leaning his elbow on a box of Kleenex. "A small bottle, please."

"Well now, let me see. A bottle of shoe-white." He ran his finger along a bewildering line of bottles on the second shelf and caught one up quickly in his hand. "Haven't sold any of this stuff since last summer. You wearin' summer shoes, young lady?"

Elin blushed and shook her head shyly. "I have to clean my skates. I'm in the Carnival tonight. How much, please?"

"Well, is that so?" The young man opened his eyes wide. "You in the Carnival, eh? I'm goin' to that Carnival. I'll watch out for you. What part you in?"

"I'm Finland." Elin smiled proudly. "I come after Chrissie and she's Czechoslovakia. How much, please?" She took off her mitten and unrolled the money from the sticky piece of brown paper.

"This'll be my treat," the young man grinned. "Then when I see Finland comin' on the ice I'll say to myself, 'Just look at that shine, Jo! You helped that little girl put that shine on her skates!'"

Elin's mouth opened a little in surprise as he wrapped the bottle. "There she is now." He handed the parcel across the counter. "Now I'll be watchin' for you tonight, Finland. You skate real good for Jo, and get a real good shine on those skates!"

Anna followed her out of the door. "Gee, Elin, did he really give you the cleaning stuff? Gee!"

Äiti was bending over Juhani when Elin opened the door, wrapping him in his warm brown snowsuit. "Now you will be a good boy while Äiti is away," she told him in Finnish, "so that Mrs. Venna will want you to come again and stay."

"Where's Isä and Grandfather?" Elin was all out of breath from running. "And where's Juhani going?"

"Isä is wash himself, Elin. He just come home from mine." Äiti hung Elin's coat close to the stove to dry. "Juhani is go over to Mrs. Venna's while we go to Carnival. And Grandfather, he is do big job in back porch. Go, look!"

Elin ran to the back door and opened it. There was Grandfather, rubbing the steel of her blades with a big, soft cloth, till it shone like Lake Ramsay in the summer sun.

"Oh, Grandfather!" Elin squatted down beside him.

"I got the stuff for cleaning the tops and I didn't have to pay anything for it either. So now I can give the money back to you."

"Eh, Elin! This is the day for you!" Grandfather stopped rubbing and laughed. "All the nice things come all together, like as always. But go now, Elin. Have the little lie-down on the bed and then the food. You will be there early at the arena for the getting-ready."

She crept downstairs after her rest and sat down at the table. "I don't think I want anything to eat right now." She eyed the mound of potatoes and carrots on her plate without interest.

"But you must eat the food, Elin. You have much work to do for all the people who see you. Eat just a little. Please? For Grandfather?"

"It's all knots inside me, Grandfather." Elin swallowed a few morsels. "I'm not even hungry."

Grandfather understood. "That is because you are little afraid now. All that will go when you start to skate."

Then it was time to leave. They all stood there while she put on her coat and hood. Äiti looked at her strangely, as if she were someone else's little girl. Isä laughed and gave her a playful spank. Grandfather leaned down to pat her on the shoulder. "Remember, little one, tonight you skate for Finland, and some day you skate for Canada."

Then she was gone out of the light and warmth of the house, and the snow whirled about her feet as she ran through the darkness.

There were a lot of people there already when she arrived at the arena. The dressing-rooms hummed with voices. Elin peeked into one of them. "Is Mrs. Wilson here yet?"

"Here I am, child. Right in here, please!" A tall lady

grasped her arm and drew her into the dressing-room.

Mrs. Wilson helped her take off her green dress. "My, oh my!" She unfolded the Finnish costume carefully. "Isn't this a pretty outfit. Did your mother make it, dear?"

Elin shook her head nervously. "My grandfather brought it for me all the way from Finland. Äiti had to shorten the skirt because it was too long for skating."

"Well, it's certainly lovely, dear, and you're just going to look sweet with that golden hair of yours." She finished lacing the black bodice with its scarlet and gold embroidery, then she called through the door. "Ettie! Another ready for make-up here!"

"Coming!" A thin little lady with a long face, and a yellow smock over her dress ran into the room, a big box in her hand. "Just sit down there, dearie." She pointed to a bench stretched along one side of the room. "Now look in that mirror and we'll start to work."

"What are you going to do, please?" Elin eyed her fearfully.

The thin lady took a big daub of cold cream and lathered it across Elin's face. "I'm going to make you look like somebody's golden-haired doll." Elin saw her smile in the mirror. "Now I'll wipe that off and put on some foundation cream." She took a heavy cream that was almost peach-coloured in the bright light of the dressing-room. "We really have to rub this stuff on smoothly."

"Do I have to have some of that red goo on, too?" Elin pointed to the little jar on the table.

"Oh yes, indeedy. That's rouge. Here, I'll put that on next." She smeared the red cream on Elin's face around the cheekbones. "Now we'll have a little on the lips. And then the powder."

"I do look like a doll now," Elin laughed. "Just like a doll Isä gave me a long time ago for Christmas."

"You're beautiful, dearie! Next please!" Another girl came to sit on the bench. Mrs. Wilson took Elin's hand and led her out into the corridor.

"All right, child. You're ready. Sit in your place on the bench and wait your turn. Joanie! Joanie!" Mrs. Wilson called to another little girl, smaller than Elin, wandering around the hallway with her costume over her arm.

Elin sat in a long line-up on the bench. Boys and girls in costume were everywhere around her. If she bent a little sideways she could see outside to the rink. The arena buzzed with people talking. *All those rows of seats out there are full now,* she thought. *There must be hundreds of people waiting to see the Carnival. And they're waiting to see me as Finland, too!*

"Don't be scared, Elin. You're wonderful!" Anna in her gay Polish dress stood up ahead of her. Elin waved. She wondered if Anna were scared, too. She couldn't ask her because she had been in another dressing-room, with Yolande and the girls who went on ahead of Elin. "Everybody here must be a little scared," she guessed. "Because everybody's mother and father, and maybe grandfather, too, are waiting out there to see the skating. Anyway," she remembered suddenly, "I can't be scared because I'm not Elin Laukka at all tonight. I'm Finland. And Finland is brave and strong!"

"Elin! Elin!" Someone was calling to her. She turned. There was Elizabeth in her glistening Canada costume, the silver crown on her head. She was eating a chocolate bar, and waving a bottle of Coca-Cola at Elin. A little girl in a golden dress like a sheaf of wheat stood beside her.

She was Saskatchewan, the wheat province of Canada. "Good luck, Elin!" they shouted.

"You better get up close to the door so you can see me!" Wendy yelled from the front of the line. "I'll be near the first!"

"Shhh! They're going to begin!"

Elin heard the band strike up the opening music. Slowly a long file of young people, their skins stained dark brown, their lithe bodies in scant Indian garb, swung out through the entrance to the rink. The story of Canada had begun, the story of how Canada had grown to be a great nation, a nation of many peoples. "The Indians are doing their war dance around the make-believe campfire now!" somebody whispered. Elin leaned as far sideways as she could to watch. Another long line began to move out across the ice, a line of Viking warriors, in short tunics with big silver-horned caps on their heads. They pushed a huge dragon ship on wheels before them, and when they set it in the middle of the ice, they danced and whirled about it in perfect formation.

"It's my turn now. Watch me, Elin!" Wendy flew out through the entrance. Elin moved closer to see. With one bound Wendy was out on the ice and . . . oh! She had fallen! Wendy had fallen flat on her face! A rush of clapping sounded from the arena above. They were clapping for Wendy even though she had fallen! Wendy bounced to her feet unabashed, grinning jauntily at the friendly faces up in the darkness. She stumbled off again across the ice.

Perhaps Finland would fall, too. Elin rubbed her skate nervously against the leg of the bench. After all, if Wendy fell, *anything* could happen!

"Say, did you hear that?" Wendy scrambled back on

the tips of her skates. "They clapped harder for me than for anybody else! Say, I guess I did all right, didn't I?" She disappeared down the corridor, jabbering to all the girls along the way.

Out on the ice dashed the great men who had lived long ago in Canada's history: John Cabot, who first touched the shores of this "new found land"; Jacques Cartier, in close breeches of bright green and a doublet of scarlet, with a little flat purple cap on his head and a small sword swinging at his side; LaSalle and the valiant explorers who had opened the doors to the Canadian wilderness; even General Wolfe with his battalion in brilliant red military coats and short skirts and pants. They did a quick march step on the ice.

On and on they filed past Elin: Laura Secord, dressed in a white cap and black and white gown, and prancing on the ice before her, her cow, a little boy with a baggy brown sack over his body. They brought a roar of laughter from the crowd. Elin's hands and feet grew cold with fear. She watched the pioneers, the girls with dolls cradled in their aprons, the boys with tiny axes swung from their shoulders and bags of grain hanging on their hips, which they pretended to scatter over the ice.

Slowly the boys and girls, representing the people of the world who had come to Canada in search of freedom and happiness, whirled out on the ice. Elin's turn was close at hand. There! Yolande had gone! A little French maiden in ruffled muslin and a high lace bonnet. England and Ireland followed and then the Scottish lass with her bright plaid skirt and bonnie tam o'shanter perched on her brown curls. One by one they went: Russia, Hungary, even Italy and faraway Greece. Suddenly there was a yawning, empty space in front of her.Czechoslovakia had gone!

Now! Elin felt her legs trembling. Would they do what she wanted them to? Then, as if he were right there beside her, she heard Grandfather's voice. *Remember, little one, tonight you skate for Finland and some day you skate for Canada.*

She took a deep, slow breath and skated out on the ice to wait her turn. The notes of "Finlandia" rose and rolled from the band at the far end of the rink. At first she saw only the vast expanse of rink before her, and the enormous maple leaf, painted in its brilliant autumn colours on the ice beneath her feet.

Suddenly a great shout boomed above the music. "Hurrah for Finland! Hurrah for Elin, mine friend!" There was no mistaking that voice. It was Mr. Kurtsheff! Elin peered up into the blobs of white faces. Every seat was occupied. She looked along the railing. There was Mr. Kurtsheff, big, fat stomach and all, waving his arms wildly. Stepan was waving, too. Elin remembered to smile at them. The nice young man from the drug store must be up there, too, looking for the shine on her skating boots.

There was the music cue to begin! When the spotlight found her she had forgotten the rows of staring faces. She remembered only Grandfather, and the joy of being a bird on silver wings. All around her she could see, in the splash of lights thrown down from the ceiling, the boys and girls of other lands forming a huge rainbow circle in which she was to do her skating. She raced up the ice and lifted her slim leg high in the air as she did the sparrow. Just as she had done on that first night of rehearsal she dipped and swayed down the ice, forgetting all but the feel of the silver skates, and the tiny song they sang as they glided over the huge maple leaf on the floor of the arena.

She swirled down the ice in a wide curving edge and whirled to a standstill in the centre. Then she began her spin. Like a big dizzy top she twirled around, one leg held up close to her body. The music swelled higher and higher. Four hundred throats gasped their admiration. Suddenly she stopped. She started to skate off up the ice again. A mighty burst of applause followed her as she swung her legs and body in the movement of the spread eagle. Her feet made one long line as she carved a circle on the ice. Swiftly she sped down toward the band in a swinging arc. Now was the moment for the half turn and the flying leap in the air! Faster! Faster! Down the rink! For a brief, happy second she soared into space. Then she drifted down to the ice again as smoothly as a floating thistledown. A quick swaying edge up the ice, another graceful sparrow, a dainty curtsey . . . it was over.

A roar of voices and clapping hands filled the air about her as she knelt there, the little skirt of red, black and yellow stripes spread around her on the ice, the scarlet embroidered bodice glistening in the spotlight, her golden hair falling like sunlight from under the tiny white lace cap.

Elin looked up at all the faces. Then she saw Grandfather, high up, near the top in the darkness, and beside him Isä and Äiti. But it was Grandfather she noticed for he was standing and he was not clapping. He looked down at her across the sea of white faces and he was smiling. Elin heard his voice in the applause that thundered through the darkness.

"It is good sometime to remember the fine thing the

Finnish blood give you. For you it has given the Sisu. My Elin know her place and is happy in it . . . *Remember, little one . . . some day you skate for Canada.*"